George sucked in a breath.

For the first time in nearly four years he and Sophy—his wife—were face to face.

Wife? Ha.

They might have stood side by side in a New York City judge's office and repeated after him. They might have a legally binding document declaring them married. But it had never meant anything more than a piece of paper.

Not to her.

Not to either of them, George told himself firmly, though the pain he felt was suddenly different than before. He resisted it. Didn't want to care. Sure as hell didn't want to feel!

The very last thing he needed now was to have to deal with Sophy.

Award-winning author **Anne McAllister** was once given a blueprint for happiness that included a nice, literate husband, a ramshackle Victorian house, a horde of mischievous children, a bunch of big, friendly dogs, and a life spent writing stories about tall, dark and handsome heroes. 'Where do I sign up?' she asked, and promptly did. Lots of years later, she's happy to report the blueprint was a success. She's always happy to share the latest news with readers at her website, www.annemcallister.com, and welcomes their letters there, or at PO Box 3904, Bozeman, Montana 59772, USA (SASE appreciated).

HIRED BY
HER HUSBAND

BY
ANNE McALLISTER

First published in Great Britain 2010
Harlequin Mills & Boon Limited,
Eton House, 18-24 Paradise Road, Richmond, Surrey TW9 1SR

© Barbara Schenck 2010

ISBN: 978 0 263 21430 7

Harlequin Mills & Boon policy is to use papers that are natural,
renewable and recyclable products and made from wood grown in
sustainable forests. The logging and manufacturing process conform
to the legal environmental regulations of the country of origin.

Printed and bound in Great Britain
by CPI Antony Rowe, Chippenham, Wiltshire

HIRED BY
HER HUSBAND

CHAPTER ONE

WHEN THE PHONE RANG that evening, Sophy grabbed it as fast as she could. She didn't need it waking Lily. Not just when her daughter had finally fallen asleep.

Lily's fourth birthday party that afternoon had exhausted them both. Normally an easygoing sunny-natured child, Lily had been wound up for days in anticipation. Five of her friends and their mothers had joined them, first at the beach and then here at the house for a cookout, followed by ice cream and cake.

Lily had been on top of the world, declaring the party, "the bestest ever." Then, in the time-honored fashion of overtired four-year-olds everywhere, she'd crashed.

It had taken a warm bath, a cuddle on Sophy's lap, clutching her new stuffed puppy, Chloe, and half a dozen stories to unwind her.

Now finally she was asleep, sprawled in her bed, but still clinging to Chloe. And, with the house a wreck all around her, Sophy didn't need Lily wide awake again. So at the phone's first shrill ring, Sophy snatched it up.

"Hello?"

"Mrs. Savas?"

The voice was a man's, one she didn't know. But it was the name she heard that gave her a jolt. Of course her cousin and business partner Natalie was now Mrs. Savas—had been ever since her marriage to Christo last year—but Sophy wasn't used to getting calls asking for Natalie at home. For a split second she hesitated, then said firmly, "No. I'm sorry. You've got the wrong number. Call back during business hours and you can speak to Natalie."

"No. I'm not trying to reach Natalie Savas," the man said just as firmly. "I need to reach *Sophia* Savas. Is this—" He paused as if he were consulting something, then read off her telephone number.

Sophy barely heard it. Her mind had stuck on *Sophia Savas.*

That had been her name. Once. For a few months.

Suddenly she couldn't breathe, felt as if she'd been punched. Abruptly she sat down wordlessly, her fingers strangling the telephone.

"Hello? Are you there? Do I have the correct number?"

Sophy took a quick shallow breath. "Yes." She was relieved that she didn't stammer. Her voice even sounded firm to her own ears. Cool. Calm. Collected. "I'm Sophia. Sophia McKinnon," she corrected, then added, "formerly Savas."

But she still wasn't convinced he had the right person.

"George Savas's wife?"

So much for not being convinced. Sophy swallowed. "Y-yes."

No. Maybe? She certainly didn't think she was still George's wife! Her brain was spinning. How could she not know?

George could have divorced her at any time in the past four years. She'd always assumed he had, though she'd never received any paperwork. Mostly she'd put it out of her mind because she'd tried to put George out of her mind.

She shouldn't have married him in the first place. She knew that. *Everybody* knew that. Besides, as far as she was concerned, a divorce was irrelevant to her life. It wasn't as if she were ever marrying again.

But maybe George was.

Sophy's brain abruptly stopped spinning. Her fingers gripped the receiver, and she felt suddenly cold. She was surprised to feel an odd ache somewhere in the vicinity of her heart even as she assured herself she didn't care. It didn't matter to her if George was getting married.

But she couldn't help wondering, had he finally fallen in love?

She had certainly never been the woman of his dreams. Had he met the woman who was? Was that why she was getting this call? Was this official-sounding man his lawyer? Was he calling to put the legal wheels in motion?

Carefully Sophy swallowed and reminded herself again that it didn't matter to her. George didn't matter. It wasn't as if their marriage had been real. She'd only hoped…

And now she told herself that her reaction was only because the phone call had caught her off guard.

She mustered a steadying breath. "Yes, that's right. Sophia Savas."

"This is Dr. Harlowe. I'm sorry to tell you, Mrs. Savas, but there's been an accident."

"Are you sure about this?" Natalie asked. She and her husband, Christo, had come over the minute Sophy had rang them. Now they watched as she threw things in a duffel and tried to think what else she needed to take. "Going all the way to New York? That's clear across the country."

"I know where it is. And yes, I'm sure," Sophy said with far more resolution than she felt. It had nothing to do with how far she was going. It was whom she was going to see when she got there. "He was there for me, wasn't he?"

"Under duress," Natalie reminded her.

"Snap," Sophy said. There was going to be a fair amount of duress involved in this encounter, too. But she had to do it. She added her sneakers to the duffel. One thing she knew from her years in New York was that she'd have to do plenty of walking.

"I thought you were divorced," Natalie said.

"So did I. Well, I never signed any papers. But—" she shrugged "—I guess I thought George would just take care of it." God knew he'd taken care of everything else—including her and Lily. But that was George. It was the way he was.

"Look," she said finally, zipping the duffel shut and raising her gaze to meet Natalie's. "If there was any way not to do this, believe me, I wouldn't. There's not. According to the papers in George's personnel file at Columbia, I'm his next of kin. He's unconscious. They may have to do surgery. They don't know the extent of his injuries. They're in 'wait and see' mode. But if things go wrong—" She stopped, unable to bring herself to voice possibilities the doctor had outlined for her.

"Sophy," Natalie's voice was one of gentle warning.

Sophy swallowed, straightened and squared her shoulders. "I have to do this," she said firmly. "When I was alone—before Lily was born—he was there." It was true and she made herself face that fact as much as she told it to her cousin. He had married her to give Lily a father, to give her child the Savas name. "I owe him. I'm paying my debt."

Natalie looked at her doubtfully, but then nodded. "I guess so," she said slowly. Then her eyes flashed impatiently. "But what kind of grown man gets run over by a truck?"

A physicist too busy thinking about atom smashing to watch where he was going, Sophy thought privately. But she didn't say that. She just told the truth.

"I don't know. I just know I appreciate your dropping everything and coming over to stay with Lily. I'll call you in the morning. We can arrange a time and do a video call, too." She patted her briefcase where she'd already packed her laptop. "That way Lily can see me and it won't be so abrupt. I hate leaving her without saying goodbye."

She had never left Lily in four years—not for more than

a few hours. Now she knew that if she woke Lily she'd end up taking her along. And that was a can of worms she didn't intend to open.

"She'll be fine," Natalie assured her. "Just go. Do what needs to be done. And take care of yourself," she advised.

"Yes. Of course. It will be fine," Sophy assured her, picking up the briefcase as Christo hefted the duffel and headed out to the car.

Sophy allowed herself a quick side trip into Lily's room. She stood there a moment just looking at her sleeping daughter, her dark hair tousled, her lips slightly parted. She looked like George.

No. She looked like a Savas, Sophy corrected herself. Which Lily was. George had nothing to do with it. But even as she told herself that, her gaze was drawn to the photo on the bedside table. It was a picture of baby Lily in George's arms.

Lily might not remember him, but she certainly knew who he was. She'd demanded to know about him ever since she discovered such people as fathers existed.

Where was her father? she'd asked. "My daddy," she said. "Who is my daddy?" Why wasn't he here? When was he coming back?

So many questions.

For which her mother had had such inadequate answers, Sophy thought miserably now.

But how could she explain to a child what had happened? It was hard enough to explain it to herself.

She'd done her best. She'd assured her daughter of George's love. She knew that much was true. And she'd even promised that some day Lily would meet him.

"When?" her daughter had demanded.

"Later." Sophy kept the promise deliberately vague. "When you're older."

Not now. And yet, at the same time Sophy thought the

words again, another thought popped into her head: What if he died?

Impossible! George had always seemed tough, impervious, imminently indestructible.

But what did she really know about the man who had so briefly been her husband? She only thought she'd known...

And what man, even a strong tough one, could fend off a truck?

"Sophy?" Natalie's voice whispered from the door. "Christo's waiting in the car."

"Coming." Quickly Sophy bent and gave her daughter a light kiss, brushed her hand over Lily's silky hair, then sucked in a deep, desperate breath and hurried out of the room.

Natalie was waiting, watching worriedly. Sophy mustered a smile. "I'll be back before you know it."

"Of course you will." Natalie gave her a quick smile in return, then wrapped Sophy in a fierce tight hug intended, Sophy knew, to supply a boatload of encouragement and support. "You don't still love him, do you?" Natalie asked.

Sophy pulled back and shook her head. "No," she vowed. She couldn't. *She wouldn't!* "Absolutely not."

They weren't giving him any painkillers.

Which would be fine, George thought, though the pounding in his head was ferocious and moving his leg and elbow made him wince, if they would just let him sleep.

But they weren't doing that, either. Every time he fell blessedly asleep they loomed over him, poking and prodding, talking in loud kindergarten-teacher voices, shining lights in his eyes, asking him his name, how old he was, who was the president.

How idiotic was that? He could barely remember his age or who the president was when he *hadn't* just got run over by a truck.

If they'd ask him how to determine the speed of light or

what the properties of black holes were, he could have answered in the blink of an eye. He could talk about that for hours—or he could have provided he was able to keep his eyes open long enough.

But no one asked him that.

They went away for a while, but then came back with more needles. They did scans, tutted and muttered, asked more of their endless questions, always looking at him expectantly, then furrowed their brows, worried, when he couldn't remember if he was thirty-four or thirty-five.

Who the hell cared?

Apparently they did.

"What month is it?" he demanded. His birthday was in November.

They looked askance when he asked them questions.

"He doesn't know what month it is," one murmured and made quick urgent notes on her laptop.

"Doesn't matter," George muttered irritably. "Is Jeremy all right?"

That was what mattered right now. That was what he saw whenever his eyes were closed—his little four-year-old dark-haired neighbor darting into the street to chase after his ball. That and—out of the corner of his eye—the truck barreling down on him.

The memory still made his breath catch. "How's Jeremy?' George demanded again.

"He's fine. Barely a scratch," the doctor said, shining a light in George's eyes. "Already gone home. Much better off than you. Hold still and open your eyes, George, damn it."

Ordinarily, George figured, Sam Harlowe probably had more patience with his patients. But he and Sam went back to grade school. Now Sam gripped George's chin in firm fingers and shone his light again in George's eyes again. It sent his head pounding through the roof and made him grit his teeth.

"As long as Jeremy's okay," he said through them. As soon as Sam let go of his jaw, George lay back against the pillows and deliberately shut his eyes.

"Fine. Be an ass," Sam said gruffly. "But you're going to stay right here and you're going to rest. Check on him regularly," Sam commanded the nurse. "Keep me posted on any change. The next twenty-four hours are critical."

George's eyes flicked open again. "I thought you said he was all right."

"*He* is. The jury's still out on you," Sam told him gruffly. "I'll be back."

As that sounded more like a threat than a promise, George wanted to say he wouldn't be here, but by the time he mustered his wits, Sam was long gone.

Annoyed, George glared after him. Then he fixed his gaze on the nurse. "You can leave, too," he told her irritably. He'd had enough questions. Besides, his head hurt less if he shut his eyes. So he did.

He may have even slept because the next thing he knew there was a new nurse pestering him.

"So, how old are you, George?" she asked him.

George squinted at her. "Too old to be playing games. When can I go home?"

"When you've played our games," the nurse said drily.

He cracked a smile at that. "I'm going to be thirty-five. It's October. I had oatmeal for breakfast this morning. Unless it's tomorrow already."

"It is," she told him.

"Then I can go home."

"Not until Dr. Harlowe agrees." She didn't look up while she checked his blood pressure. When she finished she said, "I understand you're a hero."

George squinted at her. "Not likely."

"You didn't save a boy's life?"

"I knocked him across the street."

"So he wouldn't get killed by a truck," the nurse said. "That qualifies as 'saving' in my book. I hear he just got a few scrapes and bruises."

"Which is what I've got," George pointed out, about to nod toward the ones visible on his arm. "So I should be able to go home, too."

"And you will," she said. "But head injuries can be serious."

Finally, blessedly, she—and all her persistent colleagues—left him alone. As the hours wore on eventually the hospital noises quieted. The rattle of carts in the halls diminished. Even the beeps and the clicks seemed to fade. Not the drumming in his head, though. God, it was ceaseless.

Every time he drifted off, he moved. It hurt. He shifted. Found a spot it wasn't quite so bad. Slept. And then they woke him again. When he did sleep it was restlessly. Images, dreams, memories of Jeremy haunted his dreams. So did ones of the truck. So did the grateful, still stricken faces of Jeremy's parents.

"We might have lost him," Jeremy's mother, Grace, had sobbed at his bedside earlier.

And his father, Philip, had just squeezed George's hand in his as he'd said over and over, "You have no idea."

Not true. George had a very good idea. There were other memories and images mingling with those of Jeremy. Memories of a baby, tiny and dark-haired. A first smile. Petal-soft skin. Trusting eyes.

She was Jeremy's age now. Old enough to run into a street the same way Jeremy had… He tried not to think about it. Tried not to think about her. It made his throat ache and his eyes burn. He shut them once more and tried desperately to fall asleep.

He didn't know how much sleep he finally got. His head was still pounding when the first glimmers of dawn filtered in through the window.

He'd heard footsteps come into the room earlier. There had been the sound of a nurse's voice speaking quietly, another low murmured response, then the sound of the feet of a chair being moved.

He hadn't opened his eyes. Had deliberately ignored it all.

All he'd thought was, please God they would go away without poking him or talking to him again. He didn't want to be poked. He didn't want to be civil.

He wanted to go back to sleep—but this time he didn't want the memories to come with it. The nurse left. The conversation stopped. Yet somehow he didn't think he was alone.

Was that Sam who'd come in? Was he standing there now, staring down at him in silence?

It was the sort of juvenile nonsensical thing they'd done as kids to try to psych the other out. Surely Sam had grown out of it by now.

George shifted—and winced as he tried to roll onto his side. His shoulder hurt like hell. Every muscle in his body protested. If Sam thought this was funny...

George flicked open his eyes and his whole being—mind and body—seemed to jerk.

It wasn't Sam in the room. It was a woman.

George sucked in a breath. He didn't think he made a noise. But something alerted her because she had been sitting beside his bed looking out the window, and now as he stared, dry-mouthed and disbelieving, slowly she turned and her gaze met his.

For the first time in nearly four years he and Sophy—his wife—were face-to-face.

Wife? Ha.

They might have stood side by side in a New York City judge's office and repeated after him. They might have a legally binding document declaring them married. But it had never meant anything more than a piece of paper.

Not to her.

Not to either of them, George told himself firmly, though the pain he felt was suddenly different than before. He resisted it. Didn't want to care. Sure as hell didn't want to feel!

The very last thing he needed now was to have to deal with Sophy. His jaw tightened involuntarily, which, damn it, made his head hurt even worse.

"What are you doing here?" he demanded. His voice was rough, hoarse from tubes and dry hospital air. He glared at her accusingly.

"Irritating you, obviously." Sophy's tone was mild, but there was a concern in her gaze that belied her tone. Still, she shrugged lightly. "The hospital called me. You were unconscious. They needed next of kin's permission to do whatever they felt needed doing."

"You?" George stared in disbelief.

"That's pretty much what I said when they called," Sophy admitted candidly, crossing one long leg over the other and leaning back in the chair.

She was wearing black wool trousers and an olive green sweater. Very tasteful. Professional. Businesslike, George would have said. Not at all the Sophy of jeans and sweats and maternity tops he remembered. Only her copper-colored hair was still the same, the dark red strands glinting like new pennies in the early morning sun. He remembered running his fingers through it, burying his face in it. More thoughts he didn't want to deal with.

"Apparently you never got around to divorcing me." She looked at him as if asking a question.

George's jaw tightened. "I imagined you would take care of that," he bit out. Since she had been the one who was so keen on it. Damn, but his head was pounding. He shut his eyes.

When he opened them again it was to see that Sophy's gaze had flickered away. But then it came back to meet his. She shook her head.

"No need," she said easily. "I certainly wasn't getting married again."

And neither was he. He'd been gutted once by marriage. He had no desire to go through it again. But he wasn't talking about that to Sophy. He couldn't believe she was even here. Maybe that whack on the head was causing him to hallucinate.

He tried shutting his eyes again, wishing her gone. No luck. When he opened them again, she was still there.

Getting hit by a truck was small potatoes compared to dealing with Sophy. He needed all his wits and every bit of control and composure he could manage when it came to coping with her. Now he rolled onto his back again and grimaced as he tried to push himself up against the pillows.

"Probably not a good idea," Sophy commented.

No, it wasn't. The closer he got to vertical, the more he felt as if the top of his head was going to come off. On the other hand, he wasn't dealing with Sophy from a position of weakness.

"You should rest," she offered.

"I've been resting all night."

"I doubt you had much," Sophy said frankly. "The nurse said you were restless."

"You try sleeping when they're asking you questions."

"They need to keep checking, you have concussion and a subdural hematoma. Not to mention," she added, assessing him slowly as if he were a distasteful bug pinned to paper, "that you look as if you've been put through a meat grinder."

"Thanks," George muttered. Yes, it hurt, but he kept pushing himself up. He wanted to clutch his head in his hands. Instead he clutched the bedclothes until his knuckles turned white.

"For heaven's sake, stop that! Lie down or I'll call the nurse."

"Be my guest," George said. "Since it's morning and I know

my name and how old I am, maybe they'll finally let me sign myself out of here and go home. I have things to do. Classes. Work."

Sophy rolled her eyes. "You're not going anywhere. You're lucky you're not in surgery."

"Why should I be?" He scowled. "I don't have any broken bones." He was half-sitting now so he stopped pushing himself up and lifted his arm to look at his watch. His arm was bare except for the intravenous tube in the back of his hand. He gritted his teeth. "Damn it. What time is it? I have a class doing an experiment tomorrow. I need to go to work." *I need to get away from this woman—or I need to grab her and hold on to her forever.*

Sophy rolled her eyes. "Like that's going to happen."

For a terrible moment, George thought she was responding to the words that had formed in his concussed brain. Then he realized she was talking about him going to work. He sagged in relief.

"The world doesn't stop just because one person has an accident," he told her irritably.

"Yours almost did."

The baldness of her statement was like a punch to the gut. And so was the sudden change in Sophy's expression as she said the words. There was nothing at all light or flippant about her now. She looked stricken. "You almost died, George!" She even sounded as if she cared.

He steeled himself against believing it, making himself shrug. "But I didn't."

All the same he knew the truth of what she said. The truck was big enough. It had been moving fast enough. If he'd been half a step slower, she would likely be right.

Would they have called Sophy if he'd died? Would she have come and planned his funeral?

He didn't ask. He knew Sophy didn't love him, but she didn't hate him, either.

Once he'd even thought they actually stood a chance of making their marriage work, that she might have really come to love him.

"What happened?" she asked him now. "The nurse said you got hit saving a child."

He was surprised she'd asked. But then he realized she might want to know why they'd tracked her down and dragged her here. It didn't have anything to do with caring about him.

"Jeremy," George confirmed. "He's four. He lives down the street from me. I was walking home from work and he came running down the sidewalk to show me his new soccer ball. He dropped it so he could dribble it, but then as he got closer he kicked it harder—at me. But it—" he dragged in a harsh breath "—went into the street."

Sophy sucked in a breath.

"There was a delivery truck coming…."

Sophy went very white. "Dear God. He's not …?"

George shook his head, then instantly wished he hadn't. "He's okay. Bruised. Scraped up. But—"

"But not dead." Sophy said it aloud. Firmly, as if to make it more believable. She seemed to breathe again, relief evident on her face. "Thank God." And her gaze lifted as if she was in prayer.

"Yes."

Then she lowered her gaze and looked at him. "Thank George."

There was a sudden flatness in her tone, and George heard an unwelcome edge of finality, of inevitability. Almost of bitterness.

His teeth came together. "What? Did you want me to let him run in front of a truck?"

"Of course not!" Sophy's eyes flashed. A deep flush of color rushed into her pale cheeks. "How could you say such a thing? I was just…recognizing what you'd done."

"Sure you were." He gave her a hard look, an expectant look, waiting for her to say the words that hung between them.

She wet her lips. "You saved him."

He almost expected it to be an accusation. She had certainly made it sound that way when she'd flung the words at him the day she'd said she didn't want to be married anymore.

"That's what you were doing when you married me," she'd cried bitterly. "You married me to *save* me!"

He had, of course. But that wasn't the only reason. Not that she would believe it. He hadn't replied then. He didn't reply now. Sophy would think what she wanted.

George stared back at her stonily, dared her to make something of it.

But whatever anger she felt seemed to go out of her. She just looked at him with those wide deep green eyes for a long moment, and then she added quietly, "You are a hero."

George snorted. "Hardly. Jeremy wouldn't have been out there running down the street at all if he hadn't seen me coming."

"What? You're saying it's your fault?" She stared at him in disbelief.

"I'm just saying he was waiting for me." He shrugged. "We kick the ball around together sometimes."

"You know him well, then? He's a friend?" Sophy sounded surprised, as if she considered it unlikely.

"We're friends." Jeremy with his dark hair and bright eyes had made him think about Lily. He didn't say that, though.

Sophy's brows lifted slightly, as if the notion that he knew who his neighbors were surprised her as well. Maybe it should. He hadn't known any of their neighbors during the few months they'd been together.

But he hadn't had time, had he? He'd been too busy finishing up the government project he was working on and trying to figure out how to be a husband and then, only weeks later, a father. The first had been time-consuming, but at least in his comfort zone.

Marriage and fatherhood had been completely virgin territory. He hadn't had a clue.

Now Sophy said, "I was surprised you were back in New York." It wasn't a question, but he assumed that she meant it as one.

"For the past two years."

"Uppsala didn't appeal?"

Ah, right. Uppsala. That was where she thought he'd gone— the job he had supposedly been up for—at the University of Uppsala in Sweden.

He couldn't have told her differently then. He hadn't been permitted to talk about it. And there was no point in talking about it now.

"It was a two-year appointment," he said.

That much was the truth. And though he could have continued to work on government projects, he hadn't wanted to. He'd agreed to the earlier one before he'd ever expected to be marrying anyone. And if things had worked out between him and Sophy, he would have bowed out and never gone to Europe at all.

When their marriage crumbled, he went, grateful not to have to stay in the city, grateful to be able to put an ocean between him and the reason for his pain.

But after two years, he'd come home, back to New York though he'd had several good offers elsewhere. "This one at Columbia is tenure track," he told her.

Not that tenure had been a factor. He'd taken the job because it appealed to him. It was research work he wanted to do, eager graduate students to mentor, a freshman class to inspire and a classload he could handle.

It had nothing to do with the fact that when he took it he'd thought Sophy and Lily were still living in the city. Nothing.

Sophy nodded. "Ah."

"When did you leave?" he asked. At her raised brows, he said, "I did drop by. You were gone."

"I went to California. Not long after you left," she said. "I started a business with my cousin."

"So I heard. My mother said she talked to you at Christo's wedding."

"Yes." Then she added politely, "It was nice to see your parents again."

George, who knew exactly what she thought of his father, said drily, "I'll bet."

He'd been invited to Christo's wedding, too. He hadn't gone because he had had no clue who his cousin Christo was marrying and no interest in flying across the country to find out. To discover later that Christo's bride was a second cousin of Sophy's blew his mind. He wondered what would have happened if he'd gone to the wedding, if they'd run into each other there.

Probably nothing, he thought heavily. There were times and places when things could happen. It had been the wrong time before. And now? Now it was simply too late.

Yet even knowing it, he couldn't help saying, "What about your business? My mother said it's called Rent-a-Bride?"

"Rent-a-*Wife*," Sophy corrected. "We do things for people that they need a second person to cope with. Things wives traditionally do. Pick up dry cleaning, arrange dinner parties, ferry the kids to dental appointments and soccer games, take the dog to the vet."

"And people pay for that?"

"They do. Very well, in fact." She met his gaze defiantly. "I'm doing fine."

Without you.

She didn't have to say the words for him to hear them. "Ah. Well, good for you."

Their gazes locked, hers more of a glare than a gaze. Then

abruptly she looked away, shifted in her chair and tried to stifle a yawn. Watching her, George realized she must have had to fly all night to get here from California.

"Did you sleep?"

She bit off the yawn. "Some." But her gaze flicked away fast enough that he knew it for the lie it was. And he felt guilty for her having been called for no reason.

"Look," he said roughly, "I'm sorry they bothered you. I'm sorry you felt you had to drop everything and fly clear across the country to sign papers. It wasn't necessary."

"The doctor said it was."

"My fault. I should have updated the contact information."

"To whom?" Her question was as quick as it was surprising. And was she actually interested in his answer?

George shrugged. "My folks. My sister, Tallie. She and Elias and the kids live in Brooklyn."

"Oh. Right. Of course." Sophy shifted in the chair, sat up straighter. "I just wondered. I thought—" But she stopped, not telling him whatever it was she'd thought, and George didn't have enough working brain cells to try to guess. "Never mind."

"I'll get it changed as soon as I get out of here," he promised.

"No problem." Sophy's easy acceptance was unexpected. At his blink of astonishment, she shrugged. "You were there for me. It's my turn."

He frowned. "So this is payback?"

She spread her hands. "It's the best I can do."

"You don't need to do anything!"

"Apparently not," she said in a mild nonconfrontational tone that reminded him of a mother humoring a fractious child.

George set his teeth. He didn't want to be humored and he damned well didn't want Sophy patronizing him.

"Fine. It's payback. So consider your debt paid," he said gruffly. He'd had enough. "Now, if you don't mind, I'd like to get some rest. And," he went on for good measure, "as you can see, I'm conscious and I can sign my own papers now. So thank you for coming, but I can take care of things myself. You don't need to hang around taking care of me. You can go."

As the words left his mouth he knew he heard the echo of almost the exact words she had thrown at him nearly four years ago: *I don't need you! I'm not a mess you need to clean up. I can take care of myself. I don't need you doing it for me. So get out of here! Leave me alone. Just go!*

And from the expression on her face, Sophy knew it, too. She looked as if he'd slapped her.

"Of course," she said stiffly and stood up, pulling her jacket off the back of the chair and putting it on.

George watched her every move. He didn't want to. But, as usual, he couldn't look away. From the first moment he'd seen her on his cousin Ari's arm at a family wedding, Sophy had always had the power to draw his gaze.

She didn't seem to notice. Something else that hadn't changed. She zipped up her jacket and picked up her tote from the floor by the chair. Then she stood looking down at him, her expression unreadable.

George made sure his was, too. "Thank you for coming," he said evenly. "I'm sorry you were inconvenienced."

She inclined her head. "I'm glad you're recovering."

All very polite. They looked at each other in silence. For three seconds. Five. George didn't know how long. It wasn't going to be enough. It never would be.

He couldn't help memorizing her even as he told himself it was a stupid thing to do. And not the first, he reminded himself grimly, where Sophy was concerned.

She gave him one last faint smile and turned away.

Her name was out of his mouth before she reached the door. "Sophy."

She stilled, glanced back, one brow lifting quizzically.

He'd thought he could leave it at that. That he could simply let her go. But he had to ask. "How's Lily?"

For a moment he thought she wouldn't answer. But then the smile he hadn't seen yet suddenly appeared on her face like the sun from behind a bank of thunderheads. Her expression softened. And she was no longer supremely self-contained, keeping him determinedly outside the castle walls. "Lily's fine. Amazing. Bright. Funny. So smart. We had her birthday party yesterday. She's—"

"Four." George finished the sentence before she could. He knew exactly how old she was. Remembered every minute of the day she was born. Remembered holding her in his arms. Remembered how the mantle of responsibility felt on his shoulders—unexpected, scary, yet absolutely right.

Sophy blinked. "You remembered?"

"Of course."

She swallowed. "Would you...like to see a picture of her?"

Would he? George nodded almost jerkily. Sophy didn't seem to notice. She was already opening her purse and taking out her wallet. She fished out a photo and came back across the room to hand it to him.

George took one look at the child in the photo and felt his throat close.

God, she was beautiful. He'd seen some snapshots that his mother had given him from the wedding so he had an idea of what Lily was like. But this photo really captured her.

She was sitting on a beach, a bucket of sand on her lap, her face tipped back as she laughed up at whoever had taken the photo. It was like seeing a miniature Sophy, except for the hair. Lily's was dark and wavy and, in this photo, wind-tossed. But her eyes were Sophy's eyes—the same shape, the same color. "British sports car green," he'd once called them. And her mouth wore a little girl's version of the delighted, sparkling grin that, like Sophy's, would make the world a brighter place. Her fingers were clutching the sides of the sand pail, and George remembered how her much tinier fingers had clutched his as she'd stared up at him in cross-eyed solemnity whenever he held her.

He blinked rapidly, his throat aching as he swallowed hard. When he was sure he could do it without sounding rusty, he lifted his gaze and said, "She's very like you."

Sophy nodded. "People say that," she agreed. "Except her hair. She has y—Ari's hair."

Ari's hair. Because Lily was Ari's daughter. Not his.

For all that George had once dared to hope, like her mother Lily had never been his.

They both belonged to Ari—always had—no matter that his cousin had been dead since before Lily's birth. Some things, George found, hurt more than the pounding in his head. He ran his tongue over his lips. "She looks happy."

"She is." Sophy's voice was firm and confident now. "She's a happy well-adjusted little girl. She's actually pretty easygoing most of the time. Once she got over the three-month mark, she stopped having colic and settled down. I managed," she added, as if it needed saying.

He supposed she thought it did. She'd had something to prove when she'd told him to get out. And she'd obviously proved it.

Now he took a breath. "I'm glad to hear it." George took one last look at the picture then held it out to her.

"You can have it," she said. "I can print another one. If you want it," she added a second later, as if he might not.

"Thanks. Yes, I'd like it." He studied it again for a long moment before turning slowly in an attempt to set it on the table next to the bed.

Sophy reached out and took it from him, standing it up

against his water pitcher so he could see it if he turned his head. "There." She stepped back again. "She can…watch over you." As soon as she said the words, she ducked her head, as if she shouldn't have. "You should get some rest."

"We'll see."

"No 'we'll see.' You should," she said firmly.

He didn't reply, and she seemed to realize that was something else she shouldn't have said, that she had no right to tell him what he should or shouldn't do. "Sorry," she said briskly. "None of my business." She turned toward the door again. "Goodbye."

He almost called her back a second time. But it would simply prolong the awkwardness between them. And when you got right down it, there was nothing else.

It had been kind of her to have come—even if it was simply "payback" on her part. Still, it was more than he would have expected.

No, that was unfair.

She might not love him, but she was tenderhearted. Sophy would do the right thing for anyone she perceived to be in need—even the man she resented more than anyone on earth.

He didn't need her, he reminded himself. He'd lived without her for nearly four years. He could live without her for the rest of his life. All he had to do was end things now as he should have done four years ago.

"Sophy!"

This time she was beyond the door and when she turned, she looked back with something akin to impatience in her gaze. "What?"

He made it clear—to both of them. "Don't worry. It will never happen again. As soon as I get out of here, I'll file for divorce."

CHAPTER TWO

OF COURSE GEORGE would get a divorce.

The only surprise as far as Sophy was concerned, was that he hadn't got one already. But even accepting the fact, Sophy felt her knees wobble as she walked away from George's room.

She moved automatically, going to fetch her duffel, which one of the nurses had allowed her to leave in a storage area near the nurses' station. But when she got there, her hands were shaking so much that she nearly brought down a load of paper supplies while trying to pull the duffel's handle out.

"Here. Let me help you." The nurse who had let her put it there in the first place took the duffel's handle, slid it out and pulled it easily out of the storage space. She tipped it toward Sophy, then looked at her closely. "Are you all right?"

"Yes, sure. Fine. Just…tired." Something of an understatement. "It's all right," Sophy murmured. "I'm fine. Truly." She did her best visibly to pull herself together so the nurse could see she was telling the truth. She shoved her hair away from her face and tried to smile. "I just need some sleep."

"Of course you do. It's been a bit traumatic. You go home now and get some sleep. Don't worry." She patted Sophy's arm. "We'll take care of your husband."

Sophy opened her mouth to correct the nurse, but what could she say? And why? Even though she wouldn't let herself think of George that way, it was impossible to lie to herself, impossible to say that walking into his hospital room had left her unaffected.

The very moment she'd laid eyes on him this morning, the years since she'd seen him fell away as if they'd never existed.

And even worse was the realization that, however desperately she might wish it, she wasn't over him at all.

When she'd walked into the hospital room to see George lying there, his head bandaged, his arm in a sling, his whisker-shadowed jaw bruised, his normally tanned face unnaturally pale, she felt gutted—exactly the same way she'd felt seeing her daughter fall off the jungle gym at her preschool.

The sight of Lily slipping and tumbling, then lying motionless on the ground, had shattered Sophy's world. That same sickening breathlessness had hit her again at the sight of George in his hospital bed.

The difference was that Lilly, having landed on wood chips that cushioned her fall, had only had the wind knocked out of her. Seconds later, she'd bounced up again none the worse for wear.

But George hadn't moved.

It was early when she'd arrived, straight from the airport, still stiff and groggy from a sleepless night on the plane. He should have been asleep. But it looked like such an unnatural sleep. And Sophy had stopped dead in the doorway, clutching the doorjamb as she stood watching him never flutter so much as an eyelash. She had been too far away to see the rise and fall of his chest.

She must have looked stricken because the nurse had said, "Watch the monitor." Its squiggly line was moving up and down jerkily. But at least it proved he was breathing because absolutely nothing else did.

"You can wake him if you want," this same nurse had said.

But Sophy had shaken her head. If George wasn't dead yet, the sight of her first thing when he opened his eyes might very well do it for him.

"No. Let him sleep," she said in a voice barely above a whisper. "I'll just wait."

"If he's not awake in an hour, I'll be back. We have to wake him regularly to see how he responds and if he remembers everything."

No doubt about his memory, Sophy thought grimly now.

She turned to the nurse. "He thinks he's going to leave today, to go to work. The doctor wouldn't really let him...."

The nurse smiled. "I don't think you need to worry about that. They'll be watching him today and probably tomorrow. You should go home now and get some rest. Come back this afternoon. Chances are he'll be much brighter by then." She gave Sophy one more encouraging smile, then checked her beeper and hurried down the hall.

Sophy stood there with her overnight bag and her briefcase and realized she didn't have a home to go to.

Home was three thousand miles away.

On the other hand, why shouldn't she go home? What was keeping her here? George had clearly dismissed her. As far as he was concerned, she needn't have bothered to come in the first place.

And she certainly wasn't going to come back this afternoon. She'd done her duty. "Payback," he'd called it.

And he'd rejected it. Consider it paid, he'd said.

That was fine with her. Shooting one last glance toward his room, she turned and wheeled her overnight bag down the hall to the elevator and pressed the button and waited, trying to keep her eyes open and stifle a yawn.

She was in the midst of the latter when the elevator door opened. There were several people in it, but only one, a young, dark-haired, very pregnant woman, swept out, then stopped dead and stared at her.

"Sophy?"

Sophy blinked, startled. "Tallie?"

"Oh, my God, it is you!" And before Sophy could do more than close her gaping mouth, George's sister, Tallie, swept her into a fierce delighted hug. "You've come back!"

"Well, I—" But whatever protest she might have made was muffled by the enthusiastic warmth of Tallie's embrace. And Sophy couldn't do much more than hug her back. It was no hardship in any case. She'd always adored George's sister. Losing the right to count Tallie as her sister-in-law had been one of the real pains of the end of her marriage.

Before she could say anything, a firm thump against her midsection had Sophy jumping back. "Was that the baby?" She looked at Tallie, wide-eyed.

Tallie laughed. "Yes. My girl likes her space." She rubbed her burgeoning belly affectionately. "This one's a girl. But more about her later. It's so good to see you." She gave Sophy another fierce hug, but was careful to move back before the baby kicked again. "George should get run over by trucks more often."

"No." Even for the pleasure of seeing Tallie again, she didn't want that.

"Well, not really." Tallie laughed with a shake of her head. "But if it brings you home—" She beamed at Sophy.

"I'm not 'home,'" Sophy said quickly. "I'm just…here. For the moment. I got a call from the doctor last night. When George was unconscious they needed his next of kin's permission for any medical procedures, and because we're not officially divorced—yet—that was me. And so—" she shrugged "—I came."

"Of course you did," Tallie said with blithe confidence. "Besides, it's about time. How is he?" Her smile faded a bit and she looked concerned. "He wouldn't let me come see him last night."

"He looks like he's been hit by a truck," Sophy said. If

Tallie hadn't seen him yet, Sophy wanted to prepare her. "Seriously. He's pretty battered. But coherent," she added when Tallie's expression turned worried.

"He flat-out refused to let us come last night. Well, there's only Elias and me around. Mom and Dad are in Santorini. And none of the boys—" her other brothers, Theo, Demetrios and Yiannis, she meant "—are here. So he was safe. He probably wouldn't have contacted me at all if he hadn't needed someone to take care of Gunnar."

"Gunnar?"

"His dog."

George had a dog? That was a surprise. "Did he rescue it?" Sophy asked.

Tallie frowned. "I don't think so. I think he got him as a puppy. Why?"

Sophy shook her head. "Never mind. I was just—never mind." She could hardly say, *Because George rescues things.* Tallie wouldn't understand.

George's sister shoved a strand of hair away from her face. "He said to go to his place and feed Gunnar, put him out and absolutely *don't* come to the hospital. He didn't need me hovering." She shook her head.

"George is an idiot," she went on with long-suffering sisterly fondness. "As if I would hover. Well, I will. But at least I waited until this morning. I'll go annoy him for a few minutes, just to let him know he can't push me around. And because the rest of the family will fuss and worry if someone hasn't set eyes on him in the flesh. But now you've come, you take the keys." She dug in the pocket of her maternity pants and thrust a set of keys into Sophy's hand.

"Me?" Immediately Sophy tried to hand them back. "They're not mine," she protested. "I can't take George's keys!"

"Why not? Because you and George are separated? Big deal."

"We're not separated! We're divorcing. I thought we already were," Sophy said. "Divorced," she clarified.

"But you're not? Good. Easier to work things out," Tallie said with the confidence of someone who had done just that and was living happily ever after. "Elias and I—"

"Were not married when you went your own ways," Sophy said firmly. "It is not the same thing. And I can't take George's keys." She tried to hand them back again, but a yawn caught her by surprise and so she ended up covering her mouth instead.

"You're exhausted," Tallie said. "How long have you been here?"

"Not that long. A couple of hours. I got into LaGuardia before dawn."

"You took a red-eye? Did you get any sleep at all?"

"Not really," Sophy admitted. "But I'm hoping I will on the way home."

Tallie looked appalled. "On the way home? What? You're going home now?"

Sophy shrugged. "He doesn't need me here. Or want me here. He made that quite clear."

Tallie snorted dismissively. "What does he know? Besides, it doesn't matter if he needs you or wants you. I do."

"You? What do you mean?"

"You, my dear Sophy, are going to save my life," Tallie told her, taking her by the arm and steering her to a pair of chairs where they could sit.

"Don't you want to see George?" Sophy said hopefully.

"In a minute. First I want to get you on your way." The CEO Tallie had once been came through loud and clear. "I need your help."

"What sort of help?"

"George, bless his heart, thinks that I can simply drop my life and take over the running of his. And admittedly, there might have been a time I could have done it," Tallie said with a grin. "But that time is not now. Not with three little boys, a baby due in three weeks, a homemade bakery business that has orders up the wazoo, orders I need to get taken care of before the arrival of my beautiful baby girl—" Tallie rubbed her belly again "—not to mention a husband who, while tolerant, does not consider sharing me with a dog for more than one night to be the best allocation of my time.

"Besides," she went on before Sophy could say a word, "he has to go to Mystic for a boat launch this afternoon. He took the kids to school, but I need to be home to get Nick and Garrett from kindergarten and Digger from preschool. I was planning to bake today before I had to go get them. And I'd take Gunnar home but he doesn't get along with the rabbit, er, actually vice versa. So—" she took a breath and gave Sophy a bright, hopeful smile "—what do you say? Will you save me? Please?"

Sophy was even more exhausted just thinking about it. She swallowed another yawn.

"And you can sleep while you're there," Tallie said triumphantly.

"George won't like it."

"Who's telling George?" Tallie raised both brows.

Not me, Sophy thought. She should say no. It was the sane, safe, sensible thing to do. The less she had to do with George or any of his family before the divorce was final, the less likely she was to be hurt again.

But life, as she well knew, wasn't about protecting yourself. It was about doing what needed to be done. "Payback" wasn't always what you thought it would be. It didn't mean you had a right not to do it.

"All right," she said resignedly. "I'll do it. But as soon as George can come home, I'm leaving."

"Of course," Tallie said, all grateful smiles. "Absolutely."

* * *

Sophy hadn't let herself think about where George might be living ever since he'd walked out of her life.

If she'd wanted to guess, she'd have picked some sterile but extremely functional apartment where he'd be called upon to do as little interaction with his environment as possible.

She couldn't have been more wrong.

George had a brownstone on the Upper West Side. Not just an efficient studio in a brownstone or even a complete floor-through apartment. George owned the whole five-story building.

And while most of the brownstones in the neighborhood had long since been subdivided into flats, George's had not.

"When he came home he said he wanted a house," Tallie told her. "And he got one."

He had indeed. And what a one it was.

Sophy stopped on the sidewalk in front of the wide stoop and stared openmouthed at the elegant well-maintained facade. It had big bay windows on the two floors above the garden entrance, and two more floors above that with three identical tall narrow arched windows looking south across the tree-lined street at a row of similar brownstones.

It had the warm, tasteful, elegant yet friendly look that the best well-kept brownstones had. And to Sophy, whose earliest memories of home were the days spent in her grandparents' brownstone in Brooklyn, it fairly shouted the word *home*.

It was exactly the sort of family home she'd always dreamed of. She'd babbled on about it to George in the early days of their marriage. He'd been preoccupied with work, of course. Not listening. At least she hadn't thought he was listening…

No, of course he hadn't been. It was coincidence.

All the same it wasn't helpful. Not helpful at all.

At least, she thought as she climbed the steps, the sound of a ferocious dog barking his head off on the other side of the front door belied any homey feelings that threatened to overtake her.

So that was Gunnar.

He sounded as if he wanted to have her for brunch.

"He's lovely," Tallie had said. "Adores George."

But apparently he wasn't keen on rabbits—except perhaps for meals—and the jury was still out on what he thought of her.

Good thing she liked dogs, Sophy thought, fitting the key in the lock and putting on her most upbeat, confident demeanor. She had no idea if it would convince Gunnar. She just hoped she convinced herself long enough to make his acquaintance.

"Hey, Gunnar. Hey, buddy," she said as she cautiously opened the door.

The dog stopped barking and simply looked at her quizzically. He was a good-size dog, all black with medium-length hair and some feathering.

"A flat-coated retriever," Tallie had told her, and when Sophy looked blank, she'd elucidated. "Think of a lean, wiry *black* golden retriever—with Opinions. Capital *O* Opinions." Gunnar's opinion of her was apparently being formed even as she talked to him.

"I hope you like me," Sophy said to him. She'd at least had the wisdom to stop at a pet shop on her way down Broadway, where she'd bought some dog treats. Now she offered one to the dog.

In her experience, most dogs took treats eagerly and without question. Gunnar took his, too. But instead of grabbing it, he accepted it delicately from her fingers, then carried it over to the rug by the fireplace where he lay down and nosed it for a few moments before consuming it.

She dragged her bag in over the threshold and shut the door behind her, then turned to survey Gunnar's—and George's—domain.

It was as impressive inside as it was out. From the mahogany-paneled entry she could see into the dining room where Gunnar was finishing his dog treat, up an equally beautiful mahogany staircase to the second floor and down a hallway to the back where a glimpse of a sofa told her she would find the living room.

But before she could go look, Gunnar came back and poked her with his nose, then looked up hopefully. "Treats are the way to your heart?" she said to him—and was surprised when he replied.

He didn't bark. He didn't growl. He just sort of—talked—made some sort of noise that had her looking at him in astonishment. So he poked her again.

"Right," she said. "Yes. Of course." And she fetched another treat out of the bag she'd bought. He accepted it with the same gravity with which he'd accepted the first one. But he didn't eat it. He simply carried it down the hall.

Sophy followed. She thought he was going to take it into the living room, which indeed was at the end of the hall. But instead Gunnar turned and went down the stairs. He obviously knew better than she did what she was supposed to be doing and was showing her where to go to open the door to the garden.

She let Gunnar out into the back garden with its cedar deck and table and chairs and the bucket of tennis balls that George must toss for Gunnar. Even though it was small and utilitarian, it was still far more appealing than the parking lot behind her apartment in California. She left Gunnar there and went back inside because she was more curious about George's office.

What would have been billed "the garden apartment" in a split-up brownstone, obviously served as George's office. One big room contained a wide oak desk, a sleek state-of-the-art computer with what was probably the biggest computer screen she'd ever seen. There were file cabinets, a worktable and shelf after shelf of scientific books. There were papers in neat stacks on the desk and worktable, and a few spread out that were filled with equations in George's spiky but very legible handwriting. When they'd been together, he had made out shopping lists in the same precise way.

Feeling a bit like a voyeur, though goodness knew she couldn't understand any of whatever he was working on, Sophy deliberately went back out into the garden and threw some tennis balls for Gunnar.

She made a friend for life. He was tireless. She was even more exhausted by the time she said, "Last one," and threw it across the small yard. Gunnar caught it on the rebound from the wall and trotted back to look at her hopefully. "Later," she promised him.

She could have sworn he sighed. But obediently he followed her back into the house, up the stairs and on up the next flight where there was a spacious yet homey family room that looked decidedly lived in—right down to the toys in one corner.

Toys?

Surprised, Sophy looked closer. Yes, there were toys. Blocks, LEGOs, Lincoln Logs and a fleet of scratched and dented Matchbox cars. Boy toys, Sophy thought. But it was clear that Tallie's boys were welcome at Uncle George's. Or did George have a lady friend with children? Not that she cared.

The family room was on the back of the house, just above the living room. Sophy found it cozy and friendly, drawing her in. There were books on the shelves, not only scientific tomes, but also popular mysteries and sailing magazines. She picked them up, noting that they weren't pristine. They had obviously been read.

She scanned the shelves curiously, then spotted a photo album as well. She opened it before she could think twice— and was quite suddenly confronted by memories that seemed almost like a blow to the heart.

The album was full of pictures from the reception after their wedding. Not the more formal portraits, but lots of casual family ones. She and George laughing as they fed each other

cake. She and George dancing on the deck of his parents'
home. She and George surrounded by his whole family, all
of them smiling and happy.

Numbly she turned the pages. After the ones from the reception, there were others of the two of them. On the beach.
In a small cozy house before a fire.

Sophy's throat tightened at the sight. At the memories of
their honeymoon.

Well, it hadn't been a honeymoon—not really. There hadn't
been time to plan one because the wedding had been so hastily
arranged and George couldn't take time off work.

All they'd had was a weekend in a tiny groundskeeper's
cottage behind one of the Hamptons mansions near his parents' home by the sea.

But for all that it had been impromptu, it had been memorable. They had, she'd thought, forged a bond that weekend.
They'd talked. They'd laughed. They'd cooked together, swum
together, walked on the beach together. They'd slept together
in the same bed—though they hadn't made love.

Her pregnancy was too far along for that.

Still, for all they'd had a less than orthodox beginning,
she'd dared to hope, to believe...

Now she shut the album and stuck it back on the shelf.
She didn't want to look. Didn't want to remember the pain of
dashed hopes, of lost love.

No, she corrected herself. It hadn't ever been love—not
really. Not to George.

Deliberately she turned away. "Come on, Gunnar," she said
to the dog. "Let's take a look at the guest room."

That's the most she was in George's house, in his life. A
guest. She needed to remember that.

"I didn't change the sheets," Tallie had apologized. "I figured I'd either be back there tonight or George would be home.
There are other rooms up above. There's a room for the boys
up there, but George probably hasn't changed the sheets since

the last time they were there. And that's where George's room is, of course."

Sophy felt enough like Goldilocks eavesdropping further in a house where she didn't belong. The last place she wanted to look at was George's bedroom.

George's bed. She didn't want to remember the nights she'd spent sharing a bed with George. Making love with George…

"I'll just take the room where you were," she'd told Tallie. "It will be fine."

It was Spartan—but perfectly adequate. It had a bed, sheets, a blanket and two pillows. What more could she ask?

Sophy kicked off her shoes and pulled off her jacket, already heading for the bed when she remembered that she needed to get on the computer and put through a video call to Natalie and Lily.

She opened her laptop on the bed and was glad she often used the video program to help out and advise the "wives" in the field who worked for her and Natalie. So she was quickly up and running, and felt an instant pang of homesickness when the call went through and she could see Lily at home with Natalie in her living room.

"Mama?" Lily demanded, sticking her face right up against Natalie's laptop. "Are you in the computer?"

Sophy laughed. "No, darling. I'm in New York. I had to come here last night, just for a couple of days. I'll be home soon. Are you being good for Auntie Nat?"

"'Course I am," Lily said. "I'm helping."

"Great." Though whether Natalie would think the help of a four-year-old was such a blessing, Sophy wasn't sure. "What are you going to do today?"

The three-hour time difference meant that Natalie and Lily were just getting started on their day. But clearly Natalie had given some thought to what they would do. Lily rattled off an entire list of things that included "after lunch going to the beach with Uncle Christo," undoubtedly so Natalie could get some real work done.

"Is that a dog?" Lily demanded, abruptly breaking off her recitation.

"Dog?" Sophy was confused, then realized that Lily wasn't just seeing her. Her daughter could see at least a part of the bedroom behind her. And Gunnar was standing by the bed looking equally curiously at the computer screen.

"Um, yes," Sophy said. "That's Gunnar."

"He's big," Lily said solemnly. "An' really, really black. Would he like me?"

"Oh, I think so," Natalie said. Gunnar, for all his ferocious barking while she was on the doorstep, had been an absolute gentleman since she'd crossed the threshold. He actually seemed to be looking at Lily.

"Hi, Gunnar," she said.

He looked quizzical and tentatively wagged his tail.

"He likes me!" Lily crowed.

"Who likes you?" Natalie reappeared and bent down to peer into the screen, eyes widening when she spotted the dog. "Who's that? Where'd he come from? Where are you?" she shot out the questions rapid-fire.

"That's Gunnar. He lives here."

"Here where?" Natalie demanded.

"At George's," Sophy said reluctantly.

"At Daddy's?" Lily demanded, sticking her face close to the screen to peer around the room eagerly. "Are you at Daddy's?"

"Yes, but—"

"Where is he?"

"Yes, where is Daddy?" Natalie demanded, frowning her concern.

Sophy heard the archness in Natalie's tone. "He's in the hospital." She tried to sound calm and matter-of-fact.

"Is Daddy okay?" Lily asked. "He's okay, isn't he, Mommy?"

"He will be," Sophy assured her.

"So what are you doing at his place?" Natalie wanted to know.

"Feeding his dog. And taking a nap. In the guest room," she added in case Natalie had other ideas.

Fortunately whatever ideas Natalie had she wasn't sharing them in front of Lily. She pressed her lips together, then shrugged and said, "Well, get some sleep then."

"I will. I just wanted to see Lily. Love you, kiddo."

"Love you, Mommy," Lily responded. "An' Daddy. An' Gunnar, too." She put her hand on the computer screen, as if she could reach out and pet him. Then she brought Chloe's face up to the screen and pointed out Gunnar to her. "He's your friend, Chloe," she told her stuffed dog. "An' he's mine, too. Oh, Uncle Christo's here. 'Bye, Mommy. 'Bye, Gunnar. See you later." And Lily skipped off, dragging Chloe away by a paw, leaving Sophy staring at the empty chair in the kitchen.

"Sorry about that." Natalie suddenly appeared. "Christo just came in bringing fresh cinnamon rolls from the bakery."

"Ah, well. A girl's got to have her priorities. Give her a hug for me."

"Of course." There was a pause. Then Natalie said, "I didn't realize Lily was quite so gung ho about George. She doesn't know him."

"She's fixated. All families have mommies and daddies. Or they're supposed to. We don't. She wanted to know why. Then she wanted to know everything about him."

"You should have told her about Ari. He's her father."

"No." Sophy didn't accept that. "He sired her. He would never have been there for her. George was."

"Briefly."

"Yes, well—" But Sophy didn't want to get into that. She

had never told Natalie all the reasons for the breakup of their marriage. It was personal. "Anyway, she asked. I told her. She's curious. It's the lure of the unknown."

Natalie looked doubtful. "What about the lure for you?"

"I'm fine," Sophy said firmly. "Besides, it's only one afternoon. I'm only putting the dog out—and grabbing a few hours' shut-eye. George isn't here. His sister asked me. I'm doing *her* a favor."

"If you say so," Natalie said doubtfully.

"I do."

"Right." Natalie shrugged, still looking concerned. "Be careful, Soph'."

"I'm being careful," Sophy replied. "Don't worry. I'll talk to you later, let you know what flight I'll be on."

"So you're coming soon?"

"Tonight. There's nothing to stay for."

Natalie smiled. "Great."

Sophy shut down the computer and put it on the nightstand by the bed. Then she finished undressing down to her underwear, drew back the covers and slid into the bed. It was heaven. And what she'd told Natalie was true: she was being careful. Very careful.

She closed her eyes and didn't let herself think about the photos in the album. She didn't let herself remember those months of hope and joy. She tried not to dwell on the fact that she was in George's house, that she could go up one more flight of stairs and lie in George's bed.

She didn't want the memories of loving him—of making love with him. She didn't want the pain.

The bed dipped suddenly. Her eyes snapped open to see Gunnar had leapt lightly onto the foot of the bed. He stood peering down at her.

She reached up and fondled his velvety soft ears, then scratched lightly behind them. He arched his back, almost like a cat. Then he turned in a circle and lay down next to her, so close that she could feel the press of his body through the covers.

She didn't know if he was supposed to be on the bed or not. She didn't care. The solid warmth of his body was comforting, reassuring. Even if he was George's dog, she liked him. She told him so.

Gunnar twitched his ear.

Sophy smiled, gave him a pat, Then shut her eyes and very carefully and resolutely did not let herself think about George. She slept.

And dreamed about him instead.

George wanted out.

Now. This afternoon.

"You can't keep me here," he told Sam, who was standing beside George's bed saying he needed to do exactly that.

Sam wasn't listening. He knew George. They'd ridden bikes together, climbed trees together and played lacrosse together. They'd even got drunk together and pounded on each other a few times—as friends do. George hadn't decided yet whether it was a stroke of good or bad luck that Sam had been the neurologist on duty when they brought him in last night.

He was leaning toward the latter right now as Sam was standing there with a stethoscope, looking grimly official.

"Well, no. I can't ground you. Or tie you to the bed," Sam agreed drily. "I did think that perhaps I could appeal to your adult common sense, but if that's a problem…"

George bared his teeth. It made his head hurt like hell. But then so did everything else he'd done today, which was pretty much nothing. He'd tried to read and couldn't focus. He'd tried to write and couldn't think. He'd tried to get up and walk around, but when he did, he'd barely made it back to the bed without throwing up. If they'd let him go home, he could at least get some sleep.

"It would be different if you didn't live alone," Sam was

saying. "Having someone who can keep an eye on you would make it more feasible."

"Babysit me, you mean," George grunted.

Sam grinned. "If the shoe fits…"

George glared. Sam just raised his brows, shrugged and looked back implacably.

Scowling, George folded his arms across his chest. "I'll be fine," he insisted. "I promise I'll call if I think it's worse."

"No," Sam said.

"I have work, a dog, a life—"

"A life?" Sam snorted at that. "I don't think so. You teach physics, for heaven's sake!"

It wasn't all he'd ever done, but George didn't go there. He just stared stonily at Sam and waited for him to give in.

"No," Sam said. "Just because I broke your nose in sixth grade doesn't mean I'm going to surrender my obligation as a doctor to give you my honest medical opinion."

"*The hell you did!* I broke *your* nose!"

Sam laughed. "Well, at least your memory's not totally shot." He lifted a hand and rubbed it ruefully across the bump in his nose. "At least I gave you the black eye."

"It wasn't that black."

"Pretty damn," Sam said. "Anyway, we'll talk about it tomorrow. We need to make sure the bleeding has stopped." He nodded toward George's head.

But George didn't notice. His attention had been grabbed by the glimpse of someone just beyond the door. *"Sophy?"*

Was he seeing things? She'd gone, hadn't she? Done her "duty" and hightailed it back to California?

But just as he thought it, she poked her head around the doorjamb. "Sorry. I didn't mean to disturb you. I thought Tallie might have come back."

Tallie? George started to shake his head, then thought better of it. "No. She went to get the boys from school. You talked to Tallie?"

Tallie certainly hadn't mentioned it. His sister had breezed in this morning to see how he was doing. Well, *breeze* might not have been the right word. *Waddle,* maybe. She'd looked as if she was going to have her baby any minute. He hadn't seen her in a month, and she hadn't been nearly that big last time he had. He felt a little guilty calling her last night and asking her to take care of the dog.

That was mostly what they'd talked about when she'd come by this morning.

"Gunnar's all taken care of," she'd assured him. "Don't worry about a thing."

She'd left again, promising to drop by later.

"Don't bother," he'd told her. It was enough that she was taking care of Gunnar. And what the hell did Sophy want with her?

"I talked to her briefly," Sophy was saying. "She came in as I was leaving. She will be back?" she asked now, as if it mattered more than a little.

"I hope not," George said. "Why?"

"I—" Sophy hesitated "—have something to give her."

"Leave it here. I'll take it home when I go. She can get it from me."

"Well, I—"

"But if it's urgent, don't bother," Sam cut in, and George realized that he'd completely forgotten about Sam, who went right on. "He's not going anywhere."

"The hell I'm not!"

Sophy looked from him to Sam and back again, her eyes wide and questioning.

"Ignore him," George said.

"Right, ignore me," Sam agreed. "I'm only his doctor."

"What's wrong with him?" Sophy was looking at Sam.

"Other than being obstinate, bloody-minded and immature?" Sam raised a brow. "Not much. Well, no, that's not true. But the rest is confidential. Patient privacy, you know? He'd have to kill you if I told you." He gave George a sly grin, then turned a far warmer one on Sophy, which was when George remembered that Sam always had had a thing for the ladies.

"Cut it out," George said with enough of an icy edge to his voice that Sam's grin faded.

His friend looked at him, then at Sophy, then back at him. "What?"

George gave him a steely look, but didn't speak.

Sam looked at him curiously, gaze narrowing speculatively. But when George still didn't say anything, he shrugged and made his move. Sticking out his hand he crossed the room toward Sophy. "Hi, pleased to meet you. I'm Sam Harlowe."

She took Sam's hand, smiled warmly back at him. "George's doctor."

"For my sins. And every once in a while—though not necessarily at the moment—his friend. And you are—?" He still had hold of Sophy's hand.

"I'm Sophy," she said. "McKinnon."

"Savas," George said flatly from the bed, loud enough and firmly enough that they both turned toward him. He raised his chin and didn't give a damn if the top of his head blew right off. "George's wife."

CHAPTER THREE

"Ex-wife," Sophy corrected instantly, staring at George in astonishment. "You do remember that, don't you?"

George folded his arms across his chest. "I remember no one has filed for divorce yet."

"You said you would. If you don't, I will," she told him fiercely, then flicked a glance at Sam Harlowe. He was, of course, watching this exchange with the fascination of a man with courtside seats at the U.S. Open.

"Well," he said briskly, smiling as he did so, "I'll just leave the two of you to discuss this, shall I? Nice to meet you, Sophy." He squeezed her hand again, then raised a brow and gave her what could only be described as an "interested" look. The smile turned into a grin. "Let me know when you get your marital status figured out."

She didn't blame him for being amused. From the outside it probably was amusing. From where she stood her marriage to George was anything but. But she managed to give Sam a wry smile in return.

"I'll do that," she said, not because she intended to, but because it would obviously annoy George.

"See you tomorrow," Sam said to George with a meaningful arch of his brows.

"Not here," George said.

"No," Sam began.

But George cut him off. "You said I could go home if I had someone to stay with me."

"You don't."

"Sophy will do it."

"I—"

George turned his eyes on her. "Payback," he said softly. "Isn't that what you came for?"

"You said—"

"I didn't know, did I?" He was all silky reasonableness now. "I thought I'd be out of here today. No problem. But Dr. Dan here—" he gave a wry jerk of his head toward Sam "—thinks I need someone to watch over me, hold my hand, wipe my fevered brow—"

"Kick your bony ass," Sam suggested acerbically.

George didn't even glance his way. He sat in the bed, the bedclothes fisted in his fingers, his unshaven jaw dark, his eyes glittering as his gaze bored into hers. "It's what you do, isn't it?"

She'd certainly like to kick his ass right now. Unfortunately she doubted that's what he meant. "What are you talking about?"

"Rent-a-Wife. It's your business," he reminded her, as if she might have forgotten. "I'll 'rent' you."

Sam goggled.

Sophy gaped. She couldn't even find words.

George could. "It's simple. Perfectly straightforward. Like I said, it's what you do. I mean, you did come and offer, but if you're going to renege on your 'payback,' fine. I'll hire you instead."

"Don't be ridiculous."

He gave her a perfectly guileless look. "Nothing ridiculous about it. It's sane, and reasonable. A suitable solution to a problem." George was in professor mode now. She wanted to strangle him.

He looked at Sam. "You did say that, didn't you?"

Sam rubbed the back of his neck. "Well, I—" And Sophy thought he might deny what George had said. But then he shrugged helplessly. "That's what I said. You can go home if you get someone to keep an eye on you. *If* you take it easy. *If* you don't do stupid stuff. No straining. No lifting. No running up and down the stairs. No hot sex," he added firmly.

"Well, damn," George said mildly while Sophy felt her cheeks burn. He gave Sam a quick smile, then turned his gaze back on her. "Dr. Dan says I can go home."

Sophy ground her teeth. He'd boxed her in. Made it impossible to say no. But, why?

It wasn't as if he wanted to be married to her. Clearly he didn't. Just this morning he'd been vowing—promising!—to file for divorce. And now? She pressed her lips together in a tight line.

"How long?" She didn't look at George, only at Sam.

"Depends," Sam said slowly, and she could see him go back into his doctor demeanor as he thought about it. "He needs to remain quiet. Besides the concussion, which he will still be feeling the effects of, he has a subdural hematoma."

He went on at length about the blood spill between the dura and the arachnoid membrane, telling her it was impossible to know how extensive the bleeding could be, that it might organize itself in five to six days, that it could take ten to twenty for the membrane to form. The longer he talked, the more detailed and technical Sam became. Sophy heard the word *seizure* and felt panicky. She heard the word *death* and her sense of desperation grew.

"Then this is no small matter," she summarized when Sam finally closed his mouth.

"No, it's not. So far he's doing so good. But we're not talking about Mr. Sensible here."

They weren't? George had always seemed eminently sensible—sensible to a fault almost—to Sophy. She looked at him, then at Sam.

"I'm giving you worst-case scenarios." Sam assured her.

"Thanks very much," she said drily.

"But it's necessary. It's why I won't let him go if he's going to be alone."

There was silence then. Sam waited for her answer. George didn't say a word, just stared at her with that "is your word good or not?" look on his face. And Sophy wrestled with her conscience, her emotions and her obligations.

"So you're saying it could be days," she said finally.

"Honestly it would be better for him to have someone around for several weeks. Or a month."

"A *month?*" Sophy stared at him, horrified.

Sam spread his palms. "The chances of him needing anything are minimal. They go down every day. As long as he doesn't do something to complicate matters. I'm just saying, if he's alone, how do we know?"

Indeed, how would they?

Oh, hell.

Sophy understood. But she just didn't like it. Not one bit. And she couldn't imagine George liking it, either. Not really. She shot him a glance now to see how he was taking Sam's news. His face was unreadable, his eyes hooded, his expression impassive. His arms were folded across his chest.

"I can't stay a month or two," Sophy said. "I have a life—and work—in California. I can't leave Lily that long."

"Bring her," George said.

"Who's Lily?" Sam asked.

"Our daughter," George answered before Sophy could.

Sam's eyes went round. His jaw dropped. "Odd you never mentioned any of this," he murmured in George's direction.

"Need to know," George said in an even tone.

Sam nodded, but he blinked a few times, still looking a little stunned as his gaze went from George to Sophy and back again.

He wasn't the only one feeling a bit shell-shocked.

All she'd intended to do was drop into the hospital long enough to give Tallie the key to George's house, say thank-you for the few hours sleep and say that Gunnar was fine. She hadn't even expected to have to talk to George again. After the way they'd left things this morning, she couldn't imagine he'd have anything more to say to her.

"There must be 'wives for rent' in New York," she said.

Sam didn't offer an opinion. He tucked his hands in his pockets and retreated into bystander mode.

"I'll rent you a wife," she offered.

"So much for payback," George murmured.

Sophy's fingers knotted into fists. "You'd be able to come home."

George just looked at her. "So you're saying you won't do it." His tone was mild enough, but Sophy didn't have to imagine the challenge in his words.

She clenched her teeth to stop herself saying the first, second and third things that came into her head. She got a grip, reminded herself that he was not himself—even though, frankly, he seemed more like himself than ever. And then she reminded herself as well that she owed him.

Ultimately she might have resented what he'd done by high-handedly proposing marriage and taking over her life.

But she'd let him.

She'd let herself be steamrolled. Had said yes because she knew George was all that Ari wasn't, that Ari—even if he'd lived—would never have been. And she couldn't even put a finger on when she realized she felt about George far differently and far more intensely than she'd ever felt about Ari.

She'd desperately wanted their marriage to work.

Finding out that she was just another obligation, one more of "Ari's messes" that George had had to clean up had hurt her far more than Ari's turning his back on her and fatherhood in the first place.

But that wasn't George's problem. It was hers.

And before she could move forward, she knew she had to do what she'd told him she'd come to do—settle her debts—even if what she was doing reminded her of the old cliché about the frying pan and the fire.

As for why George wanted her to do it when he didn't want to be married to her, well, maybe she'd find an answer to that. Maybe, please God, there would finally be some closure.

She straightened. "Fine. I'll do it."

Sam's eyes widened. George didn't blink.

"But only for a month—or less if possible." She met his gaze steadily. "Then we're even."

He wanted to just walk out then and there.

To get out of bed, dress and stroll out of the hospital as if he'd just spent the night in a not very pleasant hotel.

Of course it wasn't as simple as that. He didn't have any clothes, for one thing. His had been shredded and bloodied in the accident and cut from his body after. Getting out of bed hurt like sin. Strolling, of course, was impossible. He was on crutches and wearing a boot to give his ankle some support.

But at least Sophy couldn't say he'd shanghaied her into staying under spurious pretenses.

What she did say, though, as he asked her to go buy him some clothes, surprised the hell out of him.

"Not necessary," she said. "I'll just go to your place and bring you some clothes back."

"My place?"

She shrugged, dug into the pocket of her pants and held up a key. "Your house. I've got a key. It's what I came to bring back to Tallie."

His jaw dropped. He had to consciously shut his mouth. But he couldn't keep it shut. He demanded, "She gave you a key to my house?"

Another shrug. "I was tired when I ran into her by the elevator. I hadn't slept all night. And she had things to do.

The kids. Baking. Stuff for Elias. She couldn't spend all day with Gunnar. So she asked me to spend the day at your place instead of at a hotel—and get some sleep at the same time. I didn't snoop around," she told him tartly.

He didn't expect she had. Why would she bother? He shrugged awkwardly. "I was just surprised."

"Yes, well, it wasn't my idea. But it was a nice bed," she allowed. "And Gunnar is lovely." She smiled the first really warm genuine smile he'd seen since she'd been here. Better even than the smile she'd given Sam.

"He's a good dog," George allowed gruffly.

Their gazes met, and there was a moment's awkward silence, probably because it was the first thing they'd agreed on since he'd opened his eyes and found her in his hospital room.

Her gaze slid away before his did. She seemed to be staring at the key in her hand.

"So, fine," George said after a moment. "Go back to my place and get me some clothes. I'll be getting signed out of here while you're gone." He told her where things were.

Sophy nodded. "I'll be back." She shook hands with Sam again on her way out. "You'll leave me lots of instructions? Things to watch for?"

"I'll make a list," Sam said. "And you can call me any-time."

Now her smile for him was as warm as the one she'd had when she talked about Gunnar.

"Take your time," George muttered.

Sophy shot him a glare and stalked out, taking her luggage and briefcase with her.

"Well, now. You never told me about Sophy," Sam said with a knowing grin.

"No need."

"Not for you maybe," Sam laughed. "Must be an interesting

history you two have. And a daughter, too? Did I ever really know you, Georgie?"

George just looked at him. "Stuff it."

"A month? You're joking." But it was clear from her voice that Natalie didn't think it was a laughing matter. "You didn't commit yourself to staying a month in New York. Did you?" she demanded.

Sophy sighed, tucking her phone between her jaw and her shoulder as she opened one of George's dresser drawers and took out boxers, a T-shirt and a pair of socks. "Hopefully not a full month. Maybe just a couple of weeks. But yes, I did. I have to, Nat."

"You don't *have* to."

Sophy shut the drawer. "All right, maybe not in the strictest sense of *have to*. But in the world I live in, I owe George."

"For what?"

"For…things. He's a good man," Sophy hedged, moving on to the closet. She didn't want to discuss this with Natalie, but she had no choice. They were business partners. If she was going to be gone three or four weeks, that would require adjustments.

Life, it seemed, was full of adjustments these days. She pulled a button-front shirt off a hanger in George's closet and took a pair of khakis off another hanger. It seemed like too intimate a thing to be doing—prowling through George's clothes—which was why she'd called Natalie while she was doing it. So she'd focus on business and not on being in George's room.

"A 'good man' doesn't explain anything," Natalie said.

So Sophy told Natalie what Sam had told her and ended with, "So he needs someone with him. To keep an eye on him. To make sure he doesn't have more bleeding."

"And you think you're the only one who can do that?"

"No, I don't think I'm the only one who can do it. But right now George does. And—" she sighed "—I need to humor him."

"Did his doctor say that?"

"No. But getting George stressed isn't going to make things better."

"And *you're* not going to get him stressed?"

Sophy gave a short laugh. "Can't promise that, sadly." She had folded the shirt and khakis and now added them to the single shoe she'd stuck into the grocery bag she'd found in the kitchen. No point in bringing the other since he had an orthopedic boot on his left foot. Then, clothes gathered, she started back downstairs. Gunnar followed her down.

"It's not about the head injury," Natalie decided.

"Maybe not," Sophy allowed. "Maybe we just need some closure."

"I thought you were already closed."

"We're not legally divorced. I told you that."

"But you haven't lived together for years, since right after Lily was born. He hasn't been around at all."

"I didn't want him around."

"And now you do?"

Sophy didn't know what she wanted. Her emotions were in turmoil, had been since the emergency room doctor's call last night. Besides, it didn't matter what she wanted. This wasn't about her.

"Of course not. I'm just being a rent-a-wife, Nat," Sophy said with some asperity. "It's what we do."

"Oh, okay," Natalie said after a long moment, and from her tone Sophy could tell her cousin wasn't exactly convinced.

"I need to do this, Nat."

"Do it then," Natalie said more convincingly. There was a pause. Then she said, "I'll bring Lily out on Saturday."

It was far more help and cooperation than Sophy had any right to expect. "You're a gem," she said, relieved beyond measure.

"I'm glad you think so," Natalie replied. "But the truth is, I want a look at the man who's playing fast and loose with your life."

The man who was playing fast and loose with her life looked like death by the time he was dressed in the clothes Sophy had brought and was leaning on a pair of crutches, waiting while she flagged down a taxi.

Fortunately one turned up almost immediately. If it hadn't Sophy would have been sorely tempted to march him right back into the hospital and suggest they rethink things.

He had taken the clothes from her with barely a word when she'd returned with them. She'd gone out to get last-minute instructions from Sam while George got dressed. And while Sam had given her a lengthy commentary complete with all the dire things that could happen, George still hadn't come out of the room when Sam finished.

When he finally had, he was white as the sheets on the bed he'd just left, and Sophy had wanted to push him right back into it.

But George had said, "Let's go," through his teeth, and so they'd gone.

He hadn't spoken again, and he still didn't say a word when the taxi pulled up and Sophy opened the door. He just got in, not without difficulty, and slumped back against the seat, eyes shut, perspiration on his upper lip, when she shut the door again and Sophy gave the driver George's address.

Because he had his eyes closed, she studied him. And the longer she did so, the more concerned she got. His breathing seemed too quick and too shallow. His knuckles were white where he clenched his fists against the tops of his thighs. With his head tipped back, she could see his Adam's apple move as he swallowed. She thought he was swallowing too much.

He didn't open his eyes or his mouth until the driver pulled up outside his place. Sophy eyed him nervously.

"Can you manage?" she asked when she opened the door.

"Yes." The word came from between his teeth.

She didn't know if he could or not, but if he couldn't, she supposed they'd deal with it then. So she got out and paid the driver, then waited as George eased himself slowly out of the car.

Inside the house, Gunnar was barking. She could see him at the bay window, his paws up on the sill as he looked at them on the sidewalk. "He's glad to see you," she said and was pleased to see George's features lighten fractionally as a faint smile touched his mouth.

"I'm glad to see him."

Getting up the stairs was a chore. He wouldn't have had a problem with the crutches if he hadn't also hurt his shoulder in his dive to get Jeremy out of harm's way. As it was, one complicated the other. Finally he thrust the crutches in her direction and said, "Just go on in. I'll get there."

As Gunnar was still barking, she did as George said, opening the door and staying out of sight so he could get up the stairs without an audience. Or at least without her. Gunnar was delighted to see her. He bounced eagerly and nosed her hands. But then he went back to the window to check on George.

Sophy went to the door to hold it open for when he finally got there, which he did at last. He looked like death.

"I know Sam said to get you to bed, but we're not doing any more stairs right now," she told him.

He didn't argue. Wordlessly he headed straight down the hall to the living room, then sank down onto the sofa as soon as he got there. Sophy ran upstairs and got the pillows off her bed and grabbed the comforter folded at the bottom of it, then hurried back down. George hadn't moved. He didn't open his eyes when she returned. The north-facing windows let in some light, but his face was in the shadows. His head rested against the back of the sofa, the skin beneath his stubbled cheeks almost white. He looked completely spent.

Sophy plumped the pillows at one end and said, "How about lying down?"

It was an indication of how bad he must feel that he didn't argue. Slowly, laboriously, wordlessly, eyes still shut, George stretched out on the sofa. She covered him with the comforter.

"Can I get you anything?"

Okay, she knew she was hovering, and he didn't like hovering. But she wanted a response. Yes, he was doing what she suggested. But she needed a word or two. It unnerved her to see him like this. It was so out of character. George took charge. George could do anything, always had.

"No," he said, lips barely moving, his voice low and a little rusty. "I'm fine."

"Of course you are," she said with a smile and tucked the comforter in around him, unable to fight the feeling of fondness—no, not simply fondness…*love,* God help her—that swamped her.

"Oh, George." She swallowed hard and blinked back sudden unexpected tears.

His eyes flicked open. "What?"

But Sophy turned her head away. "Nothing. I'm going to get you some water." She started toward the kitchen.

"I don't need water," she heard him say.

"Well, I need to get it," she replied, not turning around. And she hurried toward the kitchen where, please God, she would get a grip.

She could not survive the coming month if she got teary-eyed at the drop of a hat.

Death didn't seem like such a bad alternative.

George was appalled at how weak he was, how badly his

head hurt—how badly *he* hurt—and how dizzy and dazed and out of control he felt.

There was no way on God's earth he could climb the stairs to his bedroom. Not now. Maybe not even today. All he wanted to do was close his eyes and lie perfectly still.

What he did not want to do was deal with Sophy.

Of course it was his own damn fault Sophy was here.

When he heard her footsteps returning, he forced his eyes open, even though as soon as he did the room began spinning again. "You don't have to stay."

"Of course I don't," Sophy said. But she made no move to leave. She set the glass on a coaster behind his head on the end table. She was so close when she bent to do it that he could smell the scent of her shampoo, enough that he could have reached up a hand and touched her. But God knew what he'd do if he did.

And George, for one, didn't want to find out.

"So go," he said with all the firmness he could manage. "You were right before. At the hospital. There are plenty of home nurses in New York. Call one."

"I don't think so."

"Sophy—"

"I'm going to put Gunnar out. C'mon, buddy," she said as if he hadn't even spoken. She snapped her fingers lightly. And George heard the clink of Gunnar's tags as the dog—*his* dog, damn it!—jumped up from beside the sofa and obediently followed Sophy down the stairs.

He didn't hear them come back.

He must have slept. He didn't know how long. The first thing he was aware of was a mouthwateringly delicious smell. The second thing was that his head didn't hurt quite as much. He moved it slowly, experimentally. The pain was still there, but less explosive now. It hurt, but not enough to make him sick to his stomach.

He cracked his eyes open.

Sophy was sitting in the recliner, her laptop on her out-stretched legs, her head bent, her burnished copper hair, almost brown in the shadows, hiding her face as she looked at the screen. He turned his head to try to see her better.

Her gaze flicked up. "Ah, you're awake. How are you doing?"

The first time he'd met her—with Ari at some cousin's wedding—George had been struck not just by her amazing hair and her pretty animated face, but by her voice. Amid what he thought of as "stage five rapids" of conversational white noise wedding chatter surging all around them, Sophy's clear soft voice had seemed like a cool still welcome pool. It still did.

He shifted his head again experimentally. "Better."

"Can I get you anything?"

He flexed his shoulders and discovered that most of his muscles were still on strike. So he said, "Maybe that water you brought earlier."

Immediately Sophy set aside the laptop and got up to fetch the glass for him. He considered saying he could get it himself, but he wasn't sure he could—not without making a production of it. So he just said, "Thank you," when she handed him the glass.

He wasn't expecting her to kneel down next to him and slide her arm under his shoulders to lift him up enough to drink easily. He let her do that, too, because it did help—and because her hair brushed his cheek and he could breathe in the scent of her just as he used to. Hers was a scent so uniquely Sophy that even if he hadn't known it was her, one breath would have taken him straight back to the night's he'd lain next to her in bed, wanting her.

Now he swallowed too quickly and choked, coughing, making his head pound once more.

Swiftly Sophy set the glass down. Her arm tightened around his shoulders. "Are you all right?"

George coughed again, wincing, then made himself nod even though it hurt. "Yeah. Just...swallowed the wrong way. I'm okay."

She eased him back down and slid her arm from beneath him. Then she sat back on her heels, her gaze intent. "Are you sure about being home, George? I can call Sam. Tell him you've changed your mind. Or he can come over. He said he'd stop by after work."

"No."

"But—"

"No! I'm not going back and Sam is not coming over. No way. Not having him here hitting on you and—"

"What?"

He gave her a derisive look. "You didn't notice Sam was just a little bit interested?"

"Interested in what?"

George stared at her. "In you!'"

"Me? Sam? Oh, don't be ridiculous. We just met. We spent five minutes talking about you and—"

"Doesn't take Sam long. He's a fast worker," George muttered. "You don't want to fool around with Sam. He's not dependable."

"I don't even know Sam."

"And now you won't have to. Got you out of there before he could work his wiles on you."

"What?" Sophy's cheeks were nearly as red as her hair. *"You got me out of there?"*

"Don't shout." George put a hand over his eyes.

"I'll shout if I want. And I'm not shouting. I'm enunciating. I don't believe you!"

George heard the sound of her standing abruptly and stalking away. He squinted to look for her, but the room began tilting again. "Just doing you a favor," he said to her back.

Sophy turned and slapped her hands on her hips. "I don't need you—or anyone—doing me favors like that!"

He looked up at her. "Just saying, you don't want to go out with Sam."

"I'll go out with whomever I damn well please!"

"Sam's a womanizer."

"Ari was a womanizer," Sophy said. "I know all about womanizers."

George went suddenly cold. Ari. It always went back to Ari. He dropped his head back on the pillows. "And that's what you want, isn't it?" he said dully. "Go away, Sophy. You're making my head hurt."

Deliberately he shut his eyes.

He refused to eat the chicken soup she made.

She told him if he didn't, she'd call Sam.

He gave her a baleful look, but when she picked up her phone and started to punch in Sam's number, George glared at her, but picked up his spoon and began to eat.

In the end he ate two bowlfuls because once he started he finished the first bowl quickly and Sophy refilled it without even asking him.

She hadn't intended to eat with him, retreating to the kitchen after she'd filled his bowl a second time. But when she didn't come back into the living room, he called after her, "Hiding in the kitchen, Soph?"

"No, I'm not hiding in the kitchen," she retorted irritably. "I'm feeding Gunnar." But then, when Gunnar finished his food and trotted happily back to be with George, she had no recourse but to bring her own bowl and return as well.

He looked a little better now. After another hour's sleep following the Sam incident, he had a bit of color in his cheeks again. He said his headache was better and the room had stopped spinning. So he had sat up on the sofa to eat and he was still sitting up now.

"It's good soup," he told her.

"Thank you," Sophy said stiffly.

"You always were a good cook."

"Thank you again."

He looked up at her. "You could sit down. A guy could get a stiff neck staring up all the time."

She wanted to say he didn't have to look at her. But instead she just sat or, to be more accurate, perched on the edge of the recliner, holding her soup bowl in one hand and her spoon in the other. But she couldn't help giving him an arch look. "Better?"

"Oh, much," George said drily, which had the effect of making her feel as if her irritation was petty and unreasonable at the same time he made her want to laugh.

Damn George could always make her laugh.

It was one of the most surprising things about him—that a man so serious, so responsible and so...so...annoyingly "right" all the time could have a certain subtle wryness that could make her stop taking herself so seriously, could make her smile, could make her laugh.

Could make her fall in love with him again.

No, oh, no. He couldn't.

Abruptly Sophy stood up. "I'm going to take Gunnar for a walk."

She didn't wait to hear what George thought about that. She just grabbed Gunnar's leash and they left. Because it was night, she took the dog over to Amsterdam Avenue and they walked south from there. Tomorrow morning, she promised him, they would go to Central Park where dogs could run off the leash before nine.

"This one isn't for you," she told him. "This walk's for me."

She needed it to give herself some space—a little more breathing room and a little less George Savas and all the feelings he evoked.

She walked briskly—Gunnar was a good pacesetter—trying to regain her equilibrium, to put her mixed-up feelings in a box and lock it up tight. This was a job. It was not a second chance. It was doing what needed to be done so she could walk away knowing that the scales were balanced, that she owed nothing more to the man who had married her.

She lectured herself all the way down to 72nd St. before she felt the adrenaline surge level off. Then they walked more sedately back while she told Gunnar all about Lily and how her daughter loved dogs. Focusing on Lily helped. And when she got back to George's she felt calmer and steadier and as if she was in control again.

The minute she opened the door and unclipped his leash, Gunnar went shooting straight for the living room. Sophy followed at a more sedate, far less enthusiastic pace.

"So," she said as she came down the hallway to enter the living room, "how's the headache now?"

George wasn't there.

CHAPTER FOUR

"GEORGE?" SOPHY BLINKED at the sight of the empty couch, as if once she did so he would suddenly rematerialize there. But no matter how many times she blinked, no George appeared.

"George!" She raised her voice a little and she poked her head in the kitchen, expecting to see him standing there, leaning on his crutches, making a forbidden cup of coffee. When she found the kitchen empty, she checked the first floor bathroom. No George there, either.

She whirled out of the bathroom and back into the living room. "George!" She yelled his name now. "Damn it, where are you?"

His crutches were leaning beside the couch. But he hadn't used them to get up the steps to the house earlier. So he'd probably taken advantage of her not being here to make his way on his own upstairs.

"Idiot," she muttered under her breath.

He could have fallen. He was the one who'd said the world was tilting earlier. She pounded up the stairs two at a time, past her own room, up to the third floor, to George's master bedroom, where she'd come to get his clothes earlier.

Then she had deliberately got in and out as fast as she could, refusing to allow herself time to look around, to imagine George in his surroundings. She'd deliberately rung Natalie so she wouldn't. And she'd barely done more than glance in the direction of his king-size bed.

Now Sophy stalked into the room and flicked on the light, hoping it made his head hurt just a little. She was glad he'd had the sense to go to bed, and at the same time annoyed that he had waited to do it until she was gone.

"Damn it, George! You can't do things like this! You've got to—"

Be careful, she was going to say.

Except there was no one to say it to. The bed was empty.

He wasn't in the adjoining bathroom, either. Nothing had changed from when she'd come up the first time. Now she did feel a shaft of concern. Surely he couldn't have had a relapse and called 911 in the half hour she had been gone, could he?

"George!" Back down the stairs she went, pausing to poke her head worriedly into the room she'd slept in just in case he'd only made it that far. But it was empty, too.

Maybe he had tried to get up, had fallen and was lying somewhere comatose.

"George!" she bellowed again when she reached the main floor, heading back toward the living room to check again.

"For God's sake, stop shouting." The disembodied voice came floating up from the garden floor office.

Sophy's teeth snapped together. She skidded to a halt, grabbed the newel post and spun around it to head down the stairs.

George was sprawled in his desk chair, staring at his oversize computer screen, reading an e-mail. Gunnar, who had obviously found him right away, looked up from where he lay at George's feet and thumped his tail.

George didn't even glance her way.

Sophy stared at him in silent fury, then stalked across the room and peered at the screen over his shoulder. "Is this all you've got open?"

"I don't multitask."

"Is it saved?"

"Of course."

"Good." She stepped around to the side of the desk and pulled the plug out of the wall. Instantly the screen went black.

"What the hell?" At least he spun his chair a half turn to look at her then—even if the action did make him wince and grab his head. "What'd you do that for?"

"I should think that's obvious. I'm saving you from yourself."

"You could have just said, 'turn off the computer.'"

"Oh? And that would have worked, would it? I don't think so." As she spoke she was methodically removing all the plugs from his surge protector, then looking around for some place to put it where he couldn't just hook it up again. Her gaze lit on the file cabinet. She opened the top drawer, dropped in the surge protector, shut the drawer, locked it and pocketed the key.

George stared at her, dumbfounded. "Are you out of your mind? I need to work. That's what I came home for."

"Well, you're not fit to work."

"Says who?"

"Says me," Sophy told him. "And Sam. You hired me to take care of you and that's what I'm doing."

"Then you're sacked."

"Throw me out. Try it," Sophy goaded him. "You can't. And I'm not leaving. I gave my word. And I keep it."

"Do you?" George said quietly.

And all of a sudden, Sophy knew they were talking about something entirely different. She swallowed and wrapped her arms across her chest. For a moment her gaze wavered, but then it steadied. She did keep her word. Always. No matter what he thought. She lifted her chin and met his gaze firmly. "Yes."

He looked as if he might argue with her. But finally he shrugged. "Maybe you do," he said enigmatically.

She didn't know what he meant by that, wasn't sure she wanted to know. She kept her arms folded, her gaze steady.

"I have to get some work done sometime, Sophy."

"Not tonight."

"My head feels better."

"Good. Not tonight."

He looked almost amused now. "Are you going to stand there and say that until tomorrow?"

"If that's what it takes." She didn't move.

George sighed and shook his head. "You're a bully."

And there was the pot calling the kettle black. She remembered so many times when she'd been expecting Lily that he had gently bullied her into taking extra good care of herself. But that was not a memory she wanted to dig into right now. Sophy just shrugged. "It's time to go to bed."

"Is that an invitation?" George's brow lifted. He grinned faintly.

"No, it's an order."

He laughed, then winced at the effect it had on his head. But finally he pushed himself slowly up out of his chair and started to hobble slowly toward the stairs. He had to pass within inches of her to get there.

She wanted to step back, to give him plenty of space, to keep her distance while he passed. Yet she sensed that if she did, he'd see it as a retreat. And Sophy was damned if she was retreating.

She stayed where she was, even looked up to meet his gaze when he reached her and stopped to loom over her, so close that if she'd leaned in an inch or two she could have pressed her lips to his stubbled jaw.

He didn't say anything, just stood there and looked down at her for a long moment. She could see each individual whisker on his jaw, trace the outline of his lips. She flicked her gaze higher to meet his eyes. He didn't speak, but the air seemed to crackle with some weird electricity between them. Sophy didn't blink.

Finally he limped slowly on toward the stairs. "Coming?" he said over his shoulder, with just a hint of sardonic challenge in his voice. "Or are you going to stay down here and set fire to my office?"

Sophy drew a breath and said with far more lightness than she felt, "Of course. I'm right behind you—ready to catch you if you fall."

It was like climbing Everest.

And he couldn't complain because if he did, Sophy would just say, "Told you so," or something equally annoying.

He couldn't even just go lie down on the couch again because when he finally got to the first floor she said, "Might as well go all the way up since you're feeling so much better. I'll get your crutches."

At least the thirty seconds it took her to do that gave him a half a minute's respite before she was standing there, holding them, saying brightly, "After you."

Serve her right if he fell on her.

He didn't. But not for lack of opportunity. Ordinarily he didn't even think about all the times he clattered up and down the flights of stairs in his house. Tonight he counted every single blasted one of them.

There were twenty per floor. It felt like a hell of a lot more. The crutches didn't help, which he already knew from his experience outside. And going down to his office hadn't been a problem. He'd eased his way down by sliding carefully on the bannister. Not that he intended to tell Sophy that!

She stayed behind him the whole way, wordlessly watching while he made the laborious climb. She never said a word, but he could sense her eyes on him.

"Don't feel you have to wait. Go right on up," he said through his teeth.

"No hurry," she replied. "I don't mind."

He did, but he wasn't telling her that, either. So he just kept on going, aware as he did so that sweat was breaking out on the back of his neck and the palms of his hands. He hoped Sophy didn't notice.

He thought she might have, though, because when they got to the second floor, she said, "Would it help if you leaned on me?"

"No, it would not." Then, realizing he'd snapped, he gritted his teeth and added, "Thank you," as lightly as he could.

Not that he wouldn't like to put an arm—hell, both arms!—around Sophy, but not now. Not this way. Not under these circumstances. He used the railing for support as he hobbled down the hall toward the next flight of the twenty thousand steps that would take him to his bedroom.

"Maybe you should just spend the night here." Sophy hovered behind him, sounding worried. "You could have this bed and—"

"You offering to share it with me?"

"No."

"Didn't think so. I'm fine." He wasn't going to admit he couldn't make it because, damn it, he could make it. He took the first step. Only nineteen thousand more to go.

In the end it probably didn't take him as long as he thought it had. All George knew was that his bed had never looked so good.

Sophy had darted around him as he'd reached the door to his room, going in ahead of him and turning down the duvet and plumping the pillows. By the time she'd finished and stepped back, he was able to ease himself down onto the mattress, all the while trying not to make it look as welcome as it was.

"Shirt," Sophy said before he could lie down.

He stared up at her and blinked. She was holding out a hand expectantly.

"You can't sleep in your clothes," she said patiently.

Of course he could. He'd done it often enough after working far into the night. But Sophy was having none of it. She knelt between his legs and unbuttoned his shirt as if he were four years old. Then she stood again and gently eased it off his shoulder, making sure she didn't hurt it any more than he'd already done hauling himself up three flights of stairs.

"Lie down," she directed.

"I thought you said I couldn't sleep in my clothes."

"You won't be." She put a hand against his chest and gave him a soft push so that he lay back against the pillows. Then she lifted his legs onto the bed and took off the orthopedic boot, his single shoe and his sock. Then she started to unbuckle his belt.

He suddenly took a much greater interest in the proceedings.

"Don't," Sophy said briskly, "think this is going anywhere."

With the disinterested efficiency of a hospital nurse, she made quick work of the belt buckle, the button and the zip.

"Lift," she commanded. And he barely had time to react before she was dragging his khakis over his hips and down his legs. She gave the duvet a shake and spread it over him, then stepped back. "There," she said, sounding satisfied. "I'll get you a glass of water. You can take one of those pills Sam sent, then you can get some sleep."

She disappeared briefly into the bathroom and returned with a glass of water and the requisite pill, which she handed to him.

"What's it for?"

"Pain."

"You didn't think to give it to me before I climbed three flights of stairs?"

"You could have asked for it," she told him. "If I'd offered, you'd have said no, wouldn't you?"

He frowned and didn't reply because, damn it, she was probably right.

Sophy grinned at him. "I thought so. You wanted to impress on me how tough you were. Besides, it might have made you dopey and I thought you would probably need all your strength to get up here."

"I could've slept on the couch," he pointed out grumpily.

"But your bed is much more comfortable."

He raised a brow. "You know that, do you?"

Sophy's cheeks reddened. "I'm speaking generically," she told him primly. "Beds are generally thought to be more comfortable than couches."

"Ah." He shifted his shoulders against the pillow. It was true. He shut his eyes and felt like he didn't quite want to open them again.

"Go to sleep," Sophy said, and for once made it sound more like a suggestion than a command. "Good night."

She started toward the door.

"Sophy."

She turned. "What?"

"Don't I get a kiss good-night?"

He was just trying to provoke her. Sophy knew that.

Because she had stood there and watched as he'd battled his way up the stairs, not going away to let him do it alone. Because she'd kept her distance and her equilibrium—barely—while taking his shirt and trousers off. Because she had almost escaped with her sanity intact.

But George wasn't going to let that happen.

"What?" she countered. "And raise your blood pressure? Sam wouldn't approve."

If anything was designed to raise his blood pressure, apparently mention of Sam was it.

The faint teasing grin instantly evaporated. George's bandaged head dropped back against the pillows and he stared at the ceiling.

"And God knows, we wouldn't want to do that," he said bitterly.

She stared at him surprised. Sam wouldn't approve. But she meant Sam in his neurologist suit. That Sam would not want his patient overdoing things. A kiss might not exactly qualify as "hot sex," but after three flights of stairs, who knew what George's blood pressure might be.

George, however, didn't seem to be thinking of Sam the neurologist, but of Sam the hypothetical womanizer.

Now it was Sophy's turn to frown. "What is it with you and Sam?" she demanded.

He turned his head slightly to look at her. "*Me* and Sam? Not a damn thing."

"Then what are you suggesting?"

"Nothing. I'm not suggesting anything."

But clearly he was. And just as clearly he wasn't going to talk about it. Sophy shook her head. "Fine. Be that way."

Then, because she wasn't going to give him the satisfaction of knowing he'd rattled her, she said, "And for what it's worth, here's your good-night kiss."

Crossing the room quickly, before she could have second thoughts, she bent down, dropped a nanosecond-long kiss on George's lips, then stepped back, smiling and, she dared to hope, unscathed.

"Good night, George," she said firmly, turned and flicked out the light.

"Not much of a kiss," he said.

She kept on going, refusing to be baited further as she tried not to notice that her lips were tingling ever so slightly.

"Sweet dreams, Sophy." His voice drifted after her as she headed down the hall to the stairs,

Shut up, George, she thought silently, scrubbing her fingers against her mouth, assuring herself that whatever she was feeling had nothing to do with kissing him.

It was just because…because…

Well, she didn't know. She couldn't think what else might have caused it, and fortunately she didn't have to because just then her mobile phone rang.

It was a local number, but one she didn't recognize. "Hello?"

"Sophy? It's Tallie. I couldn't reach George on his cell phone. So I called the hospital and they said *his wife* had taken him home." His sister sounded surprised to say the least.

"It wasn't my idea," Sophy protested. Then she explained what the doctor had told them. "He wouldn't let George go unless someone came with him. So George hired me."

"*Hired* you?"

"Well, that's what he called it," Sophy said. "Don't worry, I'm not letting him pay me. I owe him, so I'm returning the favor and paying him back."

"I'm sure George doesn't think of it that way."

Sophy was hard-pressed to articulate what George thought. All he did was confuse her—and try to run her life.

"At least you're staying! That's wonderful. We'll have you over. Of course Lily will be coming. When?"

It was a given that she would be staying long enough for her daughter to come as well, Sophy noted.

"On Saturday," she said. "My cousin is bringing her."

"Great. We'll have you over. Elias can grill. Or if George can't do that much yet, we'll bring food and come by your place."

"His place," Sophy corrected. "He's still pretty battered," she felt compelled to say. "He needs calm and quiet right now."

"We'll wait until you say you're ready then," Tallie decided. "This is such good news," she went on eagerly. "Wait till the folks hear."

"No!" Sophy said quickly and more forcefully than she should have. "I mean, they're a long way away. You don't want to tell them about George's accident. They'll worry. And I don't want you telling them I'm here, either," she said firmly.

There was a pause, as if Tallie's thoughts had finally caught up with the eager wheels turning in her brain. "Yes," she agreed, suitably subdued. "You're probably right. Better not say anything until it's settled."

"Tallie!" Sophy protested. "This is not a reconciliation. I'm here for the short-term. I live in California. George lives here. We're getting divorced."

"You could change your mind." Tallie wasn't going to give up.

"Good night, Tallie," Sophy said firmly. "I'm going to bed. It's been a long day."

She took a quick shower, then put on the elongated T-shirt she'd brought to sleep in, brushed her teeth, washed her face and had just turned back the duvet on the bed when her phone rang again.

Again it was a local number, but not the same one. Surely Tallie wouldn't be calling her back to continue the conversation on another phone. No. Tallie was determined, but she would know when to back off.

George?

Sophy felt her heart quicken. But she hadn't given him her number. She probably should have, she realized, so he could call her if he needed her.

She punched the talk button. "This is Sophy."

"Hey, it's Sam." She could actually hear him smiling.

And while she liked him and had felt comfortable with him, she felt herself stiffen. Was he, as George had suspected, calling her up to hit on her?

"Hi," she said cautiously.

"Checking on my patient," Sam said. "Figured I'd get a straighter answer from you than from him."

Sophy breathed again, feeling foolish. "He's alive. Grumpy. Annoying. I took the dog for a walk at one point and while I was gone he went downstairs to his office to work."

"You're going to have to keep an eye on him."

"I will," Sophy said, feeling guilty.

"Tonight. All night."

"What do you mean, all night?"

"If he were at the hospital, he'd be on monitors. And he'd have someone awake and checking on him regularly. You don't need to be awake, but you do need to wake up and check on him regularly. And you need to be right there."

"There?" Sophy said warily.

"Wherever he is."

"In bed."

"Perfect. Wake him every couple of hours. Make him talk to you. Be sure he makes sense. Call me if there are any problems. Do what you have to do."

And just like that, Sam was gone.

Sophy stood there and stared at the phone in her hand, feeling a strange compelling urge to throw it across the room. Then she felt another urge to pretend she hadn't got the call at all, to just crawl into bed and forget it. She could set her travel alarm and go up and check on George every couple of hours like Sam said.

Yes, and what if he needed her?

He wouldn't call her. Not if he needed her. He was too bloody-minded to admit he needed help. But what if he really did?

"Oh, blast," she muttered and, pulling on her lightweight travel robe, then dragging the duvet and her pillow with her, she climbed the stairs to George's room.

It was dark. It was silent. He was probably sound asleep.

She hoped to God he was. She padded over to the near side of the bed and began to make herself a nest on the floor.

"What the hell are you doing?"

So much for him being asleep. She kept right on making her nest. Gunnar came over to see what she was doing. "I'm sleeping here."

"On the floor?" George rolled onto his side and peered down through the darkness at her. "Are you out of your mind?"

"Sam called. He said I'm supposed to stay with you. Keep an eye on you," she corrected herself immediately.

"Did he?" George sounded all of a sudden in far better humor. "Good old Sam."

Sophy snorted. "Right. Good old Sam." She sat down on the duvet. It had felt warm and fluffy on top of her on the bed. It felt flat and thin between her and the floor. At least she'd be awake to wake him up.

"Don't be an idiot. Get up here and share the bed."

"I'm fine." She wrapped the duvet around her and snuggled down with her head on her pillow. Gunnar stuck his nose down and poked her cheek. She reached out a hand and scratched his ear.

"Sophy."

"I'm fine," she said.

"Like I was fine climbing all those damn stairs."

"Exactly." She kept her back turned and snuggled farther down. Damn this floor was hard.

George said a rude word and Sophy heard the bed creak. She ignored it. She ignored him—until she realized he had got up and was dragging the duvet off his bed and throwing it down on the floor beside her.

She rolled over and sat up in the darkness to see his white T-shirt in the moonlight as he eased himself off the bed and down onto the floor beside her!

"What on earth do you think you're doing?"

White shoulders shrugged. "Being as stupid as you are." He stretched out on the crumpled duvet. "Which is pretty damn stupid," he muttered. "God, this floor is hard."

Sophy grunted. "Then get on the bed. You need to be on the bed, George."

"It's up to you," he said.

She glared. She grumbled. She wished she could just say, *Fine, stay there,* and let him be as uncomfortable as she was. But she doubted that was what Sam had had in mind when he'd said to keep an eye on George tonight.

"And here you are again, making me do what you think is best for me," she pointed out.

"And sometimes I'm even right," he said mildly.

Which, damn it, was actually true.

"Fine." She flung back her duvet and scrambled to her feet, flung her duvet onto his bed and plopped down on top of it to glare at him, which might have been more effective if she could really have seen him and not just the shape of him in the darkness.

"Ah, sanity rears its ugly head." George grunted and tried to shove himself up as well. It was harder for him. Served him right, Sophy thought. But then guilt smote her. He was only in this shape because he'd saved a child's life, because he'd put his own life on the line.

"Give me your hand." She offered hers.

Immediately he gripped it, his long hard fingers wrapping around hers as he tried to lever himself up. It was more complicated that she imagined. He didn't have his boot on, so had to be careful of his ankle as well as his shoulder.

"I can't believe you did this." She shifted to get a better grip, had to move in to slide an arm around him to get enough leverage to get him to his feet. "Of all the stupid—"

"Your fault," he reminded her. But as she could hear the words hissing through clenched teeth, she didn't think he was enjoying it.

Neither was she. Having her arm around George's hard body, being so close she could smell the hospital soap, the disinfectant and something male that she remembered as quintessentially George unnerved her more than she wanted to admit. She shoved, hauled, hoisted.

And at last he stumbled to his feet.

"Don't do that again." His arm was over her shoulders and hers, still wrapped around him, allowed her to feel the thundering of his heart.

"I won't if you won't," he said, a catch in his breath.

She didn't answer that. It didn't merit a reply. Wordlessly she edged him over to the bed. He sat. Gunnar put his chin on George's knee. Sophy picked up his duvet and spread it over the bed, then pulled it back so he could lie down.

Then, because she knew he'd just do something stupid again if she didn't get in bed, too, she went around and slid beneath the duvet on the far side. There had to be at least two feet separating them. Plenty as long as they were awake.

But asleep she didn't trust herself.

Like Lily, she had a homing instinct for the nearest warm body. And she didn't want to wake up and find herself in George's arms.

"Told you it was a big bed," George said gruffly.

But not big enough, Sophy thought. "Gunnar," she said. "Here, Gunnar."

It didn't take any urging. In a second she felt the bed move and Gunnar's black form appeared, looming in the moonlight, looking up at them from the foot of the bed.

"For God's sake," George muttered.

"You've never let him on the bed? Oh, right. Tell me another." Sophy patted the space between them, and Gunnar instantly obliged, lying down there and heaving a contented sigh.

George made a disgruntled huffing sound.

"Just be glad you're home," Sophy said. "You could still be in the hospital."

"Promises, promises."

"If you want to go back, I'll call Sam."

"I'll bet Sam wouldn't think much of the dog in my bed."

Sophy smiled. "Sam said to do what I had to do. I'm just following instructions. Good night, George. I'll wake you in a couple of hours. Wake me if you need anything."

She rolled onto her side away from him. Away from Gunnar. It was the best she could do. She wondered if she would get a wink of sleep before it was time to wake him again.

It was a shock the next time she opened her eyes to see that it was morning and worse to discover that the warm body she was snuggled against wasn't covered with black fur.

CHAPTER FIVE

GEORGE KNEW THE MOMENT Sophy woke up.

Her breathing changed tenor. And as she realized where she was, her muscles tensed, her body stiffened. And then her eyes flicked open with something akin to horror.

He steeled himself against giving a damn. "He left," he said, refusing to apologize, refusing to pull back, or make any effort at all to untangle their limbs. Yes, no doubt he would regret it later. But right now he wasn't sorry. And right now he was staying right where he was.

"He?" There was an infinitesimal pause while she computed that, and then realized who he was talking about. "Gunnar." And as she said his name, Sophy was already moving, pulling away, putting space between them.

George didn't hold on to her. He let her go as if it didn't matter to him in the least.

"What time is it?" Sophy demanded. She jerked up to a sitting position and raked her fingers through her long tangled hair, making his fingers itch to do the same thing.

While she'd slept, he'd breathed in the crisp fresh scent of her shampoo, the scent of Sophy herself, and when several long, silken strands of hair had fallen across her face he'd been unable to help himself, and had stroked it slowly back. His hand had lingered, wanting to let his fingers play in her hair, to bury his nose in the silky tresses.

"It's a little before eight." George nodded at the clock on the dresser across the room.

Sophy glared at it as if it had let her down. "I was supposed to wake you up during the night!"

She scrambled out of the bed now and shot another hard accusatory look at Gunnar. He'd been curled up on the area rug. But now, seeing Sophy up and moving, he got up and stretched and wagged his tail at her.

"I can't believe I slept all night."

"You were tired," George said. "You said you hadn't slept much on the plane. You needed your rest. And you must have been comfortable," he suggested.

Now the glare focused on him. She didn't reply, either. She gave her head a little shake, as if she was still trying to make sense of what had happened. Then she shrugged, folding her arms across her chest, denying him the view of her breasts braless beneath the extra-long T-shirt she had slept in.

It still gave him a nice view of her legs halfway up her thighs, though, so he wasn't complaining. He studied them, remembering the sleek smoothness of those legs when they'd tangled with his. Desire had stirred then. It hadn't entirely disappeared now.

Sophy followed his gaze, realized what he was looking at and abruptly bolted out of the room.

"Damn it," George said mildly as she pounded down the stairs. He looked at the dog, who was watching him. "When she comes back she's going to be all proper and bossy," he said.

Gunnar came over to the bed and poked George with his nose. George in turn scratched him behind his ears. It was part of their morning routine. Life hadn't been exactly routine since Sophy had shown up.

"Thanks for leaving last night," George said to the dog. "Appreciate it," he added, as if Gunnar had done it on purpose.

Well, probably he had, because once George was sure Sophy was asleep, he had lain there periodically tapping the dog on the foot.

Gunnar didn't like his feet messed with. He twitched them. He shifted. And, finally, just as George hoped he would, Gunnar got up and jumped down onto the rug beside the bed. Then, unless Sophy's sleep habits had changed, it was just a matter of waiting.

George had waited.

He was used to waiting. With Sophy he felt as if he'd been waiting forever. In fact he was so tired that he fell asleep waiting.

But sometime in the middle of the night he woke up to discover Sophy was curled against him. Her arm lay across his waist, her face was pressed against his shoulder. And if he turned his head, he could touch her hair with his lips.

If?

No "if" about it. He turned to her instinctively. And when she had kept right on sleeping, he'd stroked her hair, had pressed his lips to her jaw, had even allowed himself a lingering kiss on her forehead.

Why not? Self-preservation was highly overrated.

But lying here now thinking about what else he would have liked to have done with Sophy was a bigger exercise in frustration than he wanted to endure. So he dragged himself up, got out of bed and hobbled across the room and got out clean underwear, khakis and a shirt.

It was a struggle to dress. Getting the T-shirt over his head was tricky because his shoulder was painful. Still, when he moved his head, the anvil in it didn't feel as if it were being pounded quite so vigorously. And while his bruises were a Technicolor marvel, they weren't worse. Once he put on a long-sleeve shirt most of them wouldn't be visible.

Nevertheless, by the time he was zipping up his khakis, his head was spinning a bit, and when he hobbled into the

bathroom to shave, he ended up gripping the edge of the countertop so he didn't fall over.

He didn't feel like shaving, but the two-plus days of dark
stubble on his jaw and cheeks were not a pretty sight. So he
ran the hot-water tap and leaned against the countertop while
he waited for it to heat up. Gradually the spinning in his head
slowed down, the water was hot enough to shave and he began
lathering his face.

He had the razor against his jaw when a voice behind him
said, "What are you doing?"

In the mirror he could see Sophy, dressed now, looking just
as prim and proper as he'd told Gunnar she would be, staring
at him. He applied the razor before he answered. "Guess."

She pressed her lips together as if he were doing it to annoy
her. He wasn't, and she must have realized it because she said,
"Be careful you don't fall over." And she turned away to start
straightening up his bed. "You'll be ready to lie down again
when you've finished."

Judging from the way the anvil banger was picking up the
tempo inside his head, George was pretty sure she was right.
Not that it mattered. "I have to teach an eleven o'clock class,"
he told her through barely moving lips.

She swung around and met his gaze in the mirror again.
"Teach? Don't be ridiculous. You need to go back to bed, not
teach a class."

He didn't answer, just turned his gaze back to the job at
hand. His fingers were none too steady. At the rate he was
going he could cut his throat. He slowed the stroke of his razor.
His head was starting to spin again. He wanted desperately to
finish up and sit down. But he was damned if he was going
to hurry, and damned if he would stop and rest while Sophy
was hovering. Instead he leaned his weight against the sink.

"The world will stop if you don't teach your class?" Sophy
said sarcastically.

"It's my job."

"Ah, yes. Duty. Responsibility." She twitched the duvet, flipping it up and letting it settle over his mattress. Her eyes shot sparks at him.

George tried to remain steady and upright. "You don't believe in them?"

"Of course I believe in them. But I also believe in sanity and common sense. Don't you?"

He started to grit his teeth but it hurt his head. "I'm only standing in front of a class. I'm not herding cattle or climbing ladders or jackhammering up the pavement."

"And you think it's that important that you go?" She met his gaze levelly. Her tone wasn't sarcastic now, but it did have its share of challenge.

"It wouldn't be the end of the world if I didn't, but I can be there, so I should be there. It's a matter of example," he explained. He expected her to scoff, but she didn't.

She pressed her lips together in a thin line. Her mouth worked and he could tell that whatever she was thinking, it wasn't cheerful. Then she sighed. "Fine. If you don't cut your throat shaving before it's time to go, we'll catch a cab."

He paused the razor halfway down his cheek. "We? What do you mean, we?"

Sophy shrugged. "If you're going, I'm going with you. It's my job."

She didn't know the first thing about George's work.

He was a physicist. She knew that. And now he taught physics, according to Tallie, at Columbia University. He had had lots of offers, his sister said, but he'd taken this one two years ago after his appointment in Sweden ended.

"I guess he had reasons to come back to New York," Tallie had said, watching Sophy for a reaction.

But Sophy couldn't think why he would have bothered other than his parents and his sister were nearby. She certainly wasn't. When she left their marriage, she'd left New York. And he hadn't taught physics when she was married to him.

He'd done something with physics. But heaven knew what. Sophy certainly didn't. He hadn't told *her*.

Ari had always said George was brilliant. Sophy knew he had a Ph.D. And the first time she'd met Socrates, George's father, when arrangements were being made for their wedding, he had made a point of telling her that George was highly sought after. He had, according to Socrates, a new job offer at a university in Sweden that he was expecting to take a few months after their marriage.

George had brushed off Sophy's questions about it. "It's not important," he'd said at the time.

It had been important to Sophy. If he had been serious about their marriage—about making it real—he would have shared that with her. It had to do with their future, after all.

But in fact he'd brushed off all her questions, not only about his new job offer, but about what he did, period, making Sophy feel out of line asking anything—as if she were intruding where she had no right.

And as far as what he taught, well, he probably had considered her too stupid to understand anyway.

It had not been a good feeling.

Maybe she *was* too stupid. Certainly physics was a far cry from early childhood education, which was what she had majored in. Well, if she was over her head, she'd simply sit there and watch him being brilliant.

Because she was going to class with him, whether he liked it or not.

George didn't argue with her. And that, more than anything, proved to her how very unlike himself he still was. He looked pained at her insistence. But he didn't tell her no. He said, "Whatever," through barely moving lips and went back to shaving.

His sullen acquiescence was all it took to convince her that she was absolutely doing the right thing by going along—provided he didn't see sense and stay home in the meantime.

"I'll make some breakfast," she said. "Gunnar's been out once. Shall I walk him?"

"If you want. I usually take him to the park in the morning," George told her. "Dogs are allowed off-leash in Central Park until nine. But it's okay if he misses a day or two. You can take him this evening…."

At least he didn't entertain the notion that he was going to be able to do that.

"Come on, then," Sophy said to Gunnar. "We'll take a quick run now. Then we'll fix breakfast. Maybe your master will have seen sense by the time we get back." Gunnar began to bounce eagerly, obviously understanding every word she said.

George snorted and went back to shaving.

But Sophy had seen how heavily he was leaning against the sink, and she knew he was bullheaded enough to fall over before he would sit down and rest while she was standing there.

"Men are idiots," she said to Gunnar as they went down the stairs together.

The dog didn't disagree.

They went for a fifteen-minute run. When they got back, she fixed scrambled eggs and toast and put out cereal as well, not sure what George would want, just using what he had in the refrigerator.

She'd been back nearly half an hour and had the table set in the dining room by the time George came downstairs As she worked, she told herself it was just like the early days of Rent-a-Wife when she didn't just do the administration but actually went out into houses and performed wifely duties as required.

Though most of her meal preparation had been dinners, more than a few times she'd been called into a house with a new baby where she'd been in charge of taking care of getting breakfast ready and the older kids off to school.

"It's just like that," she told Gunnar, feeling calm and professional.

But the minute George appeared in the doorway to the dining room things weren't businesslike and impersonal anymore.

And seeing him now, leaning heavily on his crutches, his smooth-shaven jaw nicked here and there with tiny razor cuts, his dark brows drawn down, the normally healthy-looking color in his cheeks now pale and strained, Sophy felt a desperate urge to run to him, to touch him, to fuss over him.

Good thing she would have had to leap the kitchen bar between them to do anything so foolish.

Clutching the edge of the countertop to anchor herself right where she stood, Sophy pasted a smile on her face. "Ah, you made it. Good. Breakfast is ready." She gestured toward the table where she'd set a place for him.

She imagined he usually ate at the bar separating the modern kitchen from the rather more formal dining area. But she didn't want him looming over her from the bar while she was working in the kitchen.

"I don't eat there," he said brusquely.

"You do today."

He shook his head. "No. It's much easier to get up and down from a bar stool than a chair at a table."

Sophy scowled, studied the situation, then sighed, annoyed that he was right. So she moved his place setting to the bar and relaid it all out for him. "All right now?" she said shortly.

"Yes, thanks." And damned if he didn't give her a smile.

George was not normally a smiler. He was far too serious, too intense. His usual expression was grave and made it hard to imagine a lighter-hearted, swoon-worthy George.

So when he did smile, it was very nearly heart-stopping. At least it always had been to Sophy.

She remembered how serious he had been when the nurse had first placed tiny minutes-old Lily in his arms. He'd looked somewhere between wooden and terrified. But then Lily had looked up at him—had tried to focus her eyes on him—and instinctively her tiny fingers had wrapped around one of his. And George had smiled such a smile!

No! Sophy spun away from the memory and jerked open the refrigerator door.

"Do you want juice?" she asked him.

"Yes, thanks."

She poured him orange juice, then started washing the pans.

"Aren't you eating?" George asked.

"I ate." And she didn't want to sit down with him, didn't want more memories to come bubbling back. "And I need to go talk to Natalie. I do have work of my own, you know."

"I know that," George said mildly, making her feel guilty for having flung her responsibilities at him. He hadn't asked her to come after all.

"Sorry, I—" She didn't finish, just shook her head and hurried out of the room, tugging her mobile phone out of her pocket as she went.

George, predictably, didn't change his mind about going to teach. So feeling rather like a Sherpa carrying his briefcase while he maneuvered his crutches, Sophy trailed after him down the steps. She thought she might have to battle him about taking a cab, but all he said when they reached Amsterdam was, "We could take the bus."

"Not today," Sophy said firmly.

He didn't reply. One point for our side, Sophy thought, waving her hand to flag a cab. She wondered if she should have fought harder to keep him home, though, when they got in the cab and he sat wordlessly, his head back against the seat, his eyes closed, all the way up to the university.

"Which building is it?" she asked him when they got close to the university.

He told her. And she told the driver so he could get them as close as possible. It was still something of a walk after they got out of the cab. George looked white. He even stopped once.

Sophy bit her tongue to keep from saying, "All right, enough."

She dogged his steps, and discovered as they got close that she wasn't the only one.

"Dr. Savas? Oh my God!" A bright-eyed blonde coed came rushing up to them as George crutched his way toward the entrance of the building. "What happened?"

She was joined almost at once by a bevy of other students—virtually all of them female—who fussed and fluttered and hovered around George, practically trampling Sophy in the process.

Bemused, she stepped back, curious to see how George would react to this display of concern, how George would react to so many women all determined to take care of him.

"Sophy!" She heard his voice suddenly ring out over the sound of feminine ooohs and awwws, and then the sea of coeds parted as he swung around on one crutch and very nearly sliced several of them off at the knees with the other until his gaze found her. Something that looked remarkably like relief passed over his features when their eyes met. And there was that smile again—maybe not as potent as it had been at breakfast, but definitely remarkable. The coeds were remarking on it, too, Sophy could tell. There was consternation and muttering going on.

Then one of the girls tossed her hair and said, "Who's *she?*" as another one answered quite audibly, "Who cares? She's old."

Sophy wasn't going to bother answering them at all. But George did.

"She's my wife," he said and shut them all up. Then he

tipped his head toward the door. "This way," he said and waited until she joined him before he nodded her ahead of him through the doors.

A trail of disgruntled coeds followed. "I didn't know he was married?" one grumbled.

"Who cares if he's married?" Sophy heard another say.

Three or four of them giggled.

George kept walking straight ahead. He looked hunted, though, by the time they got to his office. She took the key from him and opened the door. "Shut it," he said when they had both gone in. And when Sophy had, he sat down heavily in his desk chair and let his head drop back.

"Wow," Sophy said, dazed. "College has changed since I went. Do they always act like you're a boy band?"

"Not always," George said. "Not recently."

So they had, apparently.

"The ones in my class think I'm tough as nails and the last instructor they ever should have taken."

"But..." Sophy prompted when he didn't finish.

He opened his eyes and shrugged wearily. "They're girls. What can I say?"

"You're implying that all girls are hormone-driven ditzes?" Sophy glared at him.

"Not all," George said, but clearly he didn't think the field of sane sensible females was overly large. "You're not," he said finally, surprising her.

About you, I was. The words were on Sophy's tongue. She didn't say them. But they were true, just as once foolishly, she had been about Ari. But the less said about her feelings in either case, the better.

"No," she said briskly. "I'm not. I can take you or leave you. Now, is there anything I can do to help?"

It was a measure of how much George had already exerted that he simply directed her to the cabinets in his office to assemble the materials he wanted for the day's class. He was demonstrating something with bottles and water and ice. She had to get the ice from a refrigerator in the common room down the hall.

"Anything else?" she asked doubtfully.

"That should do it." George settled his crutches under his arms and led the way to his classroom. And Sophy, with her arms full of bottles and ice and a jug of water, trundled along behind, feeling more Sherpalike than ever.

George in the classroom was a revelation.

There was none of the ivory-tower professor about him— and none of the tough-as-nails teacher he'd assured her he was. Oh, she was quite sure he had high standards and his students had to work hard to meet them. But he engaged them immediately—charmed them at the same time he taught them.

While they were concerned about his injury, he didn't let them dwell on it. "I'm here, aren't I?" he said brusquely. "Let's get to work."

And nine-tenths of the girls might have been infatuated with him, and all of the students might have wanted to impress him, but George was focused on physics—and on making physics come alive for them.

They were a freshman class, Sophy began to understand. Not the crème de la crème of the postgrad population, but the eighteen- and nineteen-year-olds who were getting their first taste. And George was determined to make it a memorable one.

Sophy knew enough about the university system to know that professors of George's status only took freshmen if they wanted to, if they cared. George cared.

When a couple of the girls turned around to give her the once-over, he said, "She's not teaching you, I am. Pay attention to me."

And when one of them said, "What's she doing here?" he gave Sophy one of his heart-stopping grins over the top of his students and said, "She's making sure I don't fall over. Aren't you, sweetheart?"

He'd never called her that before, and she knew he was only saying it for effect. But she couldn't quite ignore the leap in the region of her heart. Still she did her best to tamp it down as she said, "That's exactly right."

And she apparently said it with enough emphasis that the girls in his class began to get the idea that coming on to George was a waste of time.

So they turned around and started paying attention to what he was actually saying as he gave them a minilecture on the topic to set the stage for the experiment to follow.

Sophy suspected that she was the only one who noted that he was hanging on to the podium so fiercely that he really might have fallen over without it. His students seemed to think he was just white-knuckled for emphasis.

After he'd set the stage and turned them loose to prove the theory he'd explained there was much sloshing of water and dropping of ice. Sophy imagined George would go sit down. But he didn't. He moved from group to group, advising, nodding, encouraging.

It was costing him, Sophy could tell. A muscle in his jaw ticked occasionally, and when he was in pain there were brackets of white around his mouth. He watched as they worked, but refrained from directing them too closely.

He shook his head at several questions, saying, "You have to figure things out on your own. It's the only way you'll really understand."

And finally, it seemed, they did.

So did Sophy. She understood about the experiment, but even more she also understood a little bit more about George.

He was everything she'd ever thought he was—strong, determined, hard-working, responsible. He didn't have to be here. He had sick leave. He could have stayed home. But he wouldn't because what he was doing mattered to him—and as long as he could remain upright, he was going to do it.

Just how long he was actually going to remain upright was debatable, Sophy thought, as after the class was over, he propped himself against the classroom wall and continued to give his students every bit of his energy and attention. But even as he spoke and listened she could see a thin film of perspiration on the bridge of his nose, and she noted the deepening grooves at the sides of his mouth.

She considered trying a tactful maneuver to extricate him from the situation, something that wouldn't make her look managing and wouldn't annoy George. But then she saw his jaw lock, the muscle tick again as he tried to focus on whatever one of the students was saying, and she decided there wasn't enough tact in the world.

"Excuse me," she said in the strong but brisk tones of the preschool teacher she'd been before she and Natalie had become Rent-a-Wife, "but time's up."

They turned to look at her, astonished. She gave them her best no-nonsense smile.

"Just doing my job," she told them quite honestly but with a confiding smile, and when they looked blank, she added cheerfully, "making sure Dr. Savas doesn't fall over."

The penny dropped, and they fell all over themselves apologizing as they helped carry the bottles and jugs back to the office while she handed George his crutches and waited until he preceded her out the door.

She expected he would chew her out as soon as the students left and they were alone again in his office. Instead he sank into his chair, bent his head, shut his eyes and said, "Thanks."

She was shocked and not a little alarmed. She wasn't used to seeing George in anything other than command mode. Now she had to resist an impulse to fuss. Instead she simply put the bottles and jugs away and tidied things up while she waited.

And worried and tried to marshal the arguments she would need to get him to see sense and go home rather than head to the lab where his grad students were working on projects.

He'd told her during the cab ride from his place that this introductory course was the only one he taught on campus. The rest of his work, overseeing their research and doing his own, took place at the university's research facility north of the city on the Hudson River. That was where he needed to go after the class, he'd told her.

Now she finished her housekeeping and sat down, knotting her fingers together and waiting for the argument to start.

George still hadn't moved. But at last, when it was obvious that she'd stopped moving around and the only sounds were from outside the building, he raised his head and opened his eyes to look at her.

Sophy, steely-eyed, looked right back, ready for battle.

Slowly a corner of George's mouth tipped up. "Why am I sure that I know what you're going to say?" he murmured.

Sophy opened her mouth, but before she could get a word out, he pushed himself up out of his chair and looked down at her.

"Let's go home," he said.

CHAPTER SIX

SHE GOT HIM HOME, but not up the stairs. He was breathing shallowly and teetering a bit by the time they reached the front door. And once inside, the couch in the living room was as far as he went.

"I'll just hang out here for a few minutes," he said, sinking down onto it with the relief of a camel driver reaching an oasis. He stretched out, sighed and was almost instantly asleep.

Sophy stared at him, taking in his unnaturally pale face and the lines of strain that still persisted around his mouth, and she worried, sure he'd overdone things, but unsure if she ought to call Sam.

"What do you think?" she asked Gunnar.

Gunnar went hopefully to the back door down to the garden, then to the front door and looked at his leash. Sophy supposed she should take him out. Their run this morning had been brief.

"This one will be brief, too," she told the dog, clipping his leash to his collar. She didn't suppose George would wake and need anything, but she didn't want to take chances.

She changed her clothes, left George a note on the coffee table in case he woke, then took Gunnar to Central Park. He looked disgusted that she didn't take off his leash. But when she ran with him along the pathway, he didn't seem to mind too much. They were gone barely half an hour. When they got back it didn't look as if George had moved.

She got her laptop from the bedroom on the second floor and brought it back down to the living room. That way she could work and keep on eye on George at the same time. That was the theory, at least.

In fact she spent far more time watching George. His body had barely moved but, as he slept, his face relaxed. He looked younger now, the bandage on his head gone, his dark hair drifting across his forehead, his cheeks still smooth from the morning shave, his lips no longer pressed tight with pain, softer now and slightly parted.

He looked the way he had when she'd first met him. Not a good thing because it stirred up all those same feelings— feelings that had been as wrong then as they were now. Then she had been "Ari's girl." Now she was George's "rented" wife.

Yes, she was still his wife in name—but only in name. There was no point in pretending anything else. Their marriage had never been real—and there was no point in sitting here staring at him now and wishing for the thousandth time that it was.

She got up deliberately and went to the back door. "Come on," she said to Gunnar.

After their run he'd been lying on the rug next to George. Now he bounded up and looked amazed. Another walk? he seemed to say.

Sophy shook her head. "No, but I need to burn off some steam."

She was losing it, she told herself. She was talking to the dog as if he knew what she was saying. Apparently, though, he did. He went to the basket by the door to the kitchen and picked up one tennis ball, then two, then looked hopefully at her. So she picked up the whole basket of them and took him out in the back garden.

She didn't know how long they were out there. She checked on George several times. He never moved. She threw tennis balls for Gunnar until it got dark.

And when they came back in, she left Gunnar to lie by the sofa while she carried her laptop into the kitchen. She could hear George from there if he needed anything. But she wouldn't have to look at him. Wouldn't have to remember.

She wouldn't let herself wish.

George slept the rest of the day.

When he finally woke briefly it was nearly eight thirty. He was about to simply go back to sleep again when Sophy insisted that he eat some dinner.

She expected he'd argue because that's what mule-headed men did. But George surprised her.

He took a couple of painkillers because his head still hurt, but then he sat up on the sofa and took the tray with the bowl of soup and the piece of fresh sourdough bread she handed him.

"I can come out to the kitchen," he protested mildly.

But when she said no, he didn't argue, just sat there and ate obediently. It made a nice change. And it was a relief to see him sitting up and actually being coherent. He'd been so exhausted and in such pain when they'd got home from his class that she'd been really worried, had given serious thought to calling Sam.

Now she was glad she hadn't. George seemed more alert. He had a good appetite, eating both the soup and the bread with relish. And Sophy lingered to watch.

But then she caught herself looking at him and wishing, and abruptly she excused herself.

"Things to do," she said. "I'll just go finish the dishes." And she hurried back into the kitchen, where she clattered determinedly around making a racket as she tried to distract her weak will and feeble powers of resistance.

She thought she was doing pretty well. Then she heard a noise behind her and turned to find George standing in the doorway holding his bowl in his hand.

"I feel like Oliver Twist," he said wryly, a corner of his mouth turning up, as he loomed over her. He looked very adult, very male and not like a poor starving waif at all. "Any second helpings?" he suggested hopefully.

"Of course." She snatched the bowl out of his hands. "You could have just called me. Why aren't you using your crutches?"

"Can't carry the bowl with them." George shrugged. "Plus, my ankle isn't broken. It's just sprained. The boot helps keep it steady. But I can go without the crutches."

"Well, you're not carrying the soup back with you," Sophy said. She turned her back and began ladling the soup into his bowl. "Go sit down."

But when she turned around, he hadn't moved. He was still standing there, still looming, still watching her, his dark hair tousled, his eyes hooded. "It's good," he said. "The soup."

"Thank you," she replied shortly, then looked expressively toward the living room again, in the hope that he would go sit back on the sofa. Instead he hobbled past her and, wincing, hitched himself up on one of the bar stools in the kitchen.

"That can't be comfortable."

"It's fine. I'll eat here," he said. "Keep you company."

Just what she needed. Sophy shrugged. "Suit yourself."

She turned away again and focused on the last of the dishes. Unfortunately there weren't a lot of them left.

"Thanks for coming along today," George said to her back.

She turned, surprised. "I enjoyed it. I never knew much about what you did."

George's mouth quirked. "I do other stuff, too."

"I'm sure. But that was interesting. I wouldn't have expected you to teach freshmen."

"I like it. They're rewarding. Some of them," he qualified. "When you can wake one or two up to see the world in a new way, you feel like you've accomplished something."

"I can see that. Did you—" she hesitated, then decided to ask "—teach freshmen in Uppsala?"

George hesitated for a moment, too, then shook his head. "No."

She thought he was going to leave it there, expected that he would because he'd always shut her out of that part of his life.

But then he said, "I didn't teach in Uppsala."

She blinked, digesting that, then nodded. "So, you did research?"

He drew a breath. "I wasn't in Uppsala. Not often."

Now she frowned. "You went there to teach. At least I assume you did. You were gone." She shook her head, then shrugged. "How do I know what you did?" she muttered.

"I was working for the government. Several governments, actually. It was a multinational effort. Top secret. Not teaching. Not Uppsala."

She stared at him. *Top secret?* "Not Uppsala," she echoed faintly.

"No." He opened his mouth again, as if he were about to say something else, but then he pressed his lips together briefly and cast his eyes down to focus on his bowl once more.

Sophy stood there, disconcerted, studying him, trying to rethink, to fit this new bit of information into the puzzle that was George. "I had no idea."

He lifted his gaze and met hers. "You weren't supposed to."

She understood that much. "You wouldn't have taken us with you," she said, understanding, too, now why he'd never talked with her about any plans for them to move. There had been no plans.

"I wouldn't have gone."

That made her blink. "What?"

"If we'd stayed together, I'd have told them no." His gaze didn't waver.

Sophy shook her head. "I don't understand at all now," she admitted.

"It was a job that came up before...before Ari died. Before we—" He gave a wave of his hand.

He didn't have to explain. She knew what he meant: before Ari's girlfriend turned up pregnant and alone, in need of a Savas rescue mission.

The memory stiffened her spine. "Another reason you shouldn't have married me," she said flatly.

George gave a quick shake of his head. "No. It was a matter of priorities." He made it sound cut-and-dried—and as if he'd made the obvious choice. "Anyway," he went on, "if we'd stayed together I would never have gone."

"Why not?"

"It wasn't a situation to take a wife and child into. It was potentially dangerous, certainly unstable. No place for dependents. I wouldn't have risked the two of you."

"But you risked yourself!"

He shrugged. "It was my job."

Duty. Always and forever, duty.

And she had just been another one, Sophy thought heavily. She turned away and went briskly back to cleaning up the kitchen, then put the leftover soup in the refrigerator. George finished his bowl and gave it to her when she held out her hand.

"It was good," he said with one of his heart-stopping smiles. "Thanks."

Sophy resisted it. "You're welcome," she said stiffly. "Are you going upstairs now?" she asked as he struggled to his feet.

"I think I will." His mouth twisted a bit ruefully. "Head's

not pounding quite so much, but I'm beat. I may have overdone it a bit today."

His admission made her eyes widen. There was something George couldn't handle? But she didn't say that.

"Can you make it on your own?" she asked. "Or do you want me to stand behind you to catch you if you fall?" She was only half-joking.

"I believe I can make it." One corner of his mouth tipped up. "I'll call if I need you."

So she let him go on his own. It didn't stop her keeping an ear out for any sounds of trouble, though. And she ventured over to peer up the staircase more than once to see how he was doing. It took him a long time, but at last the stairs stopped creaking and she didn't hear him anymore. Sophy didn't know how George felt after his climb, but she breathed a sigh of relief when he was up the stairs.

"Come on," she said to Gunnar, who jumped right up. "Let's go out one last time."

She didn't take him for another walk. They'd get up and go to the park in the morning early, she promised him. He seemed almost to sigh, but he went out back willingly enough. Sophy went out with him. If she stood in the garden and stared up at the windows, she could see the light on up in George's bedroom. There was, every once in a while, a shadow as he moved slowly around the room and passed in front of the lamp.

"He needs to lie down," she said to Gunnar.

Gunnar looked hopefully at his bucket of tennis balls.

"Tomorrow," Sophy promised him. "Let's go in now." When they had, she shut off the lights, picked up her laptop and climbed the stairs, Gunnar bounding on ahead to wait at the top of the stairs.

She put the laptop on the bed in the second-floor room, the one she'd used the day she'd arrived—the one she'd use again tonight because she certainly would be sleeping with George again.

She even flipped it open and turned it on, thinking she'd get some work done because it wasn't all that late yet. She might give Natalie a call and perhaps get a chance to see Lily on a video call before her daughter went to bed.

But before she did that, she should check and make sure George was settled. She didn't know what on earth he was hobbling around for. He needed to go to bed. And if he needed something, she didn't want him calling her while she was on the phone. So she climbed the stairs and went down the hall to George's room.

"Do you need anything?" she began—and stopped dead.

There was George—in all his muscular naked glory—on his way to the shower.

A slow grin spread across his face. "You could wash my back."

Sophy blushed.

George loved it when she blushed.

In four years he had never forgotten the way her eyes snapped with emotion and her cheeks grew redder than her hair. It was rewarding when her normally quick wits seemed—for the merest instant—to desert her. He reveled in it.

She didn't turn and run. No. She stopped in the doorway, her fingers lightly touching each side of the doorframe as she let her gaze rove over him. Then she said slowly, still considering him, "Now there's an idea."

He knew her tone wasn't soft and sultry intentionally. It didn't have to be. It sent a shaft of longing straight through him. And it was certainly no secret which part of him found the words most enticing.

Now it was his turn to feel his face burn. Face, hell. It wasn't his *face* that felt as if it was going up in flames.

George cleared his suddenly parched throat, then casually

turned and limped as nonchalantly as possible into the bathroom where he'd left the shower running.

"Right this way," he suggested over his shoulder. He only hoped his voice didn't sound as rusty as it felt.

He stepped into the shower, shut the door behind him and waited. And waited. Hoped against hope.

But he wasn't really surprised when minutes passed and Sophy didn't come and open the shower door and step in behind him.

He had turned the water on to let it warm up when he'd first come upstairs. He'd decided on the way up that a nice hot shower would soothe his aching body and make him feel better.

Now he thought that cold water—*ice water*—would have been a damn sight smarter.

Still, if he turned the tap to cold right now, while his ardor might fade, his muscles would seize up and his head would start pounding again. Hell of a choice. The proverbial rock and hard place, he thought, and groaned at the appropriateness of the cliché.

Served him right for still wanting her, he thought and tried to will his body into quiescence. His body had other ideas. They wouldn't go away.

Finally, deliberately he leaned forward, braced one palm against the tile beneath the shower head, and put the other on the tap. Then, as the water sluiced down his body, he gradually but inexorably turned it all to cold.

He stayed there until he could stand it no longer. Then he yanked the towel off the top of the door to scrub at his eyes before he stepped out. His teeth were chattering, his head was hammering and his whole body was rigid with cold.

"What on earth is the matter with you? You're blue!"

George jerked the towel away from his face and found himself staring into Sophy's wide eyes. They looked as shocked as he felt.

He clamped his teeth together because he'd have stuttered if he'd tried to speak.

Sophy had no such problem. She put out a hand and touched his arm, then frowned. "You're as cold as ice," she accused him.

Better than the alternative.

"I'm fine," he said. "It's all right."

"Of course it's not all right! I thought you were supposed to be smart! Why on earth would you take a cold shower and—oh!" The bright spots of color were back in her cheeks with a vengeance again, and Sophy was opening and closing her mouth like a fish.

George smiled wryly at her.

"Men!" she fumed.

"Pretty much," George agreed. He snagged another towel off the rack and hitched it around his waist. "You could leave," he suggested. "Unless you want to solve the problem another way."

For a rare and amazing moment, he thought she almost considered it. Then she gave a quick shake of her head and began backing toward the door.

"I'll wait outside," she said. "Don't fall over." She ran her tongue quickly over her lips, Then, as if a three hundred per-cent explanation were required, she added, "That's what I was doing in here. Making sure you didn't."

George grinned. "And here I thought you'd changed your mind and come to scrub my back."

Sophy rolled her eyes. But the color was back in her cheeks and he thought she ran her tongue over her lips as she shut herself firmly on the other side of the door.

For a moment George stood staring at it. Then he shook his head. The woman was a walking mass of contradictions. She came close, she backed away. She told him to get out of her life. She came clear across the country when he was hurt.

She hovered over him as if he mattered to her. Then she went cool and distant in the blink of an eye.

It was no wonder his head hurt, George thought as he dried his body slowly and carefully. And it was irritating as hell that he'd suffered through that damned cold shower because its effect had been instantly nullified by his body's reaction to Sophy's unexpected presence.

Still he wasn't apt to disgrace himself when he finally finished pulling on his boxers and a clean T-shirt, then opened the door to his bedroom.

Gunnar was lying in the middle of the bed. He lifted his head and thumped his tail happily.

Sophy, damn it, was nowhere to be seen.

CHAPTER SEVEN

JUST WHAT SHE NEEDED, Sophy thought, flinging herself onto her back on the bed—an image of a lean, muscular, stark-naked George Savas indelibly emblazoned on the insides of her eyelids!

Eyelids, ha. She had the image burned right into her retinas. Probably branded on her brain.

It wasn't fair!

Even as she thought it, she knew she was whining like a plaintive four-year-old. But it was true.

She was only here trying to make things square between them—to do *her* duty—just as George, by marrying her, had done what he misguidedly perceived to be his. It was a responsibility. A job—because George had even "hired" her, though she'd be damned if she would let him pay her a cent. She was doing this to pay him back. She didn't want his money.

Mostly she didn't want to be tempted. She didn't *want* to want George again.

It was bad enough to have lost her heart to him once. Four years ago she had believed that however inauspicious the beginning of their relationship had been, they could love each other.

She had already been well on her way to loving him by their wedding day.

Strong and stalwart and dependable, George was the exact

opposite of his cousin. The only things George and Ari had in common were some of their genes and their gorgeous good looks. But while Ari knew how to use his looks to his advantage—and did!—George seemed unaware of his. And while Ari had been there when things were fun and frivolous, George had been there when she'd needed him. Always.

She'd met him while she was dating Ari, had even danced with him at Ari and George's cousin Gregory's wedding. In fact George had been drafted in as an usher because he and Ari were the same size and he could wear Ari's tux when Ari hadn't showed up on time.

"It's not like they weren't going to have the wedding without me." Ari had dismissed the matter when Sophy had fretted about them arriving late.

That had certainly been true enough. In fact, Gregory and his bride were already man and wife by the time she and Ari had arrived.

Ari had shrugged. "Works for me. Anyway, they had George. He'll do." Ari had given his cousin a light punch on the arm. "Good old George."

Later, when she'd danced with George at the reception, she'd apologized for their tardiness even though it hadn't been her fault.

George had just shrugged and said wryly, "That's Ari. Not exactly Mr. Dependable."

At the time Sophy had still been a bit starry-eyed about Ari Savas. He was fun and flirtatious and he had charm to spare. He'd got her into bed, hadn't he? And then he'd left three days later to go skiing out west and she hadn't seen him for a month. She had written to him when she found out she was pregnant, but he'd never replied. And when next she saw him, he seemed surprised that she would have bothered to tell him.

That was the way it was with Ari. He had little interest in anyone else—and none at all in becoming a father.

Sophy got the message. In fact, because he'd bailed on her and their incipient child, she'd been tempted not to go to his funeral three months later. There didn't seem any point.

Eventually she'd decided to go because she thought that someday their child would ask about his or her father.

While Sophy was under no illusions about Ari's fidelity or love by this time, she'd once, however foolishly, cared about him. She knew she would love their child. And she owed it to that child to be able to share what she could of the man who had fathered him or her.

It was a huge funeral for a popular young man who had died before his time. All of Ari's family had been there. Most of them had paid no attention to her. She was just another one of Ari's many girlfriends. The last girlfriend, perhaps, but not a member of the family.

Only George had made a point of coming over to her afterward, taking her hand in his and not just accepting her condolences, but offering his own sympathy to her.

His lean handsome face and tousled dark hair reminded her of Ari, but the resemblance to his cousin stopped there. Ari had always been the life of the party and probably would have been even at a funeral. George was quiet and self-possessed. There was a remoteness about him even though, as they talked, Sophy was aware of his jade-green gaze boring into hers.

They didn't talk long and she never mentioned her pregnancy. It was winter. She was wearing a heavy coat, and at just five months along, she wasn't yet as big as the house she would become before Lily's birth. So George had had no idea. None of his family had. If Sophy had ever imagined that Ari might have proudly proclaimed—or even quietly admitted—he was going to be a father, she knew that day that he'd never said a word.

She'd felt a little bereft as she was leaving, and it must have showed on her face because George had drawn her into his arms and given her a hard, steadying hug. It had felt so good, so supportive, so right that Sophy had wanted to lean into it, to draw strength from it.

From George.

But fortunately common sense had prevailed and she had stepped back, decorum prevailing.

Still he'd held on to her hands. "Take care of yourself." His voice had been like rough velvet. Stronger than Ari's. Deeper.

Sophy had nodded, exquisitely aware of her hands being chafed and squeezed lightly between George's strong fingers.

"Yes," she said, throat tightening. "Yes. You, too."

She'd given him a watery smile, then desperately pulled her hands out of his and fled before sudden tears from God knew what complicated emotions spilled over onto her cheeks.

She'd hung on to that memory of George to get her through the days and weeks that followed. She told herself it was because he reminded her of Ari—but not Ari as he'd been, but rather the man she'd wanted him to be. If this child was a boy, she'd told herself, she hoped he'd be more like George than like Ari.

Not that she had a lot of time to think about either one of them. She had been teaching at a preschool-cum-day-care, a fun but exhausting job, and every day she came home more tired than the last. She loved the children, but as she'd grown bigger and the baby had become more active, simply getting through the day took a lot out of her.

When she went home after school, she had longed for a bit of adult conversation, just someone to be there. But there was none because a few weeks before Ari's funeral, her roommate, Carla, had accepted a job in Florida and moved out.

After Carla had moved, Sophy hadn't looked for another roommate right away. She was nesting and she'd liked having the space to herself. Her cousin Natalie in California, the only relative she was very close to, had suggested Sophy come out there when she'd learned Sophy was expecting.

With her parents dead and no siblings, Sophy was on her own. But while she appreciated Natalie's suggestion, she wasn't ready to take it.

"No. My doctor's here. I'm taking prenatal classes here. My job is here. I want to finish out the school year."

But her West Village apartment was expensive, and while she might have liked to live there alone, she wasn't going to be able to keep it if she didn't make an effort to find a new roommate soon.

So she put an ad up in the faculty room at the preschool and at the gym where she went to her prenatal classes. She got calls. Several of them. Most were not at all what she had in mind. But one seemed possible. A second-grade teacher named Melinda, with a four-year-old boy and a parrot, was looking for a place to live.

Sophy wasn't sure about the four-year-old or the parrot, but she imagined Melinda wasn't sure about a newborn, either, so one afternoon in early May she invited Melinda over to talk and see the apartment.

She'd just put the last of the dishes away and was sweeping the floor, hoping to impress Melinda with her housekeeping skills, when the doorbell rang.

A glance at her watch told Sophy that Melinda was half an hour early. But better early and eager than late or not at all. Besides, if the place wasn't pristine, there was no point in pretending to be something she was not. So she stuck the broom in the closet, pasted on her best welcoming smile and opened the door.

It wasn't Melinda.

It was George.

George? Sophy felt suddenly breathless. Her knees wobbled. She stared at him, words failing her.

George didn't speak at once, either. He just stood there,

lean and rugged and as gorgeous as ever, looking down at her
with those smoky green eyes of his. They held her gaze for
a moment, then slowly, inexorably slid southward so that she
could almost feel them touching her full breasts and her now
very noticeably pregnant belly. It wasn't winter any longer,
and she wasn't wearing a coat—only a loose smock that did
nothing to conceal her shape. Sophy gripped the doorknob
so tightly her hand hurt. She didn't move.

She didn't see shock in his gaze so much as curiosity and
then something like confirmation. Confirmation?

George's jaw tightened briefly as his gaze lingered on her
belly. But then it eased as his gaze traveled back up to meet
hers.

"You are pregnant." It even sounded like a confirmation.

Sophy ran her tongue over dry lips. She nodded. "Yes."
She was strangling the doorknob now. But she met his gaze
steadily. She had nothing to hide. And it was far too late for
George to say what Ari had already said: "What are you going
to do about it?"

It had to be apparent to him what she intended to "do about
it"—she intended to have it, welcome it. In fact the baby's
cradle was clearly visible in the living room behind her.

But he didn't question that. He simply asked, "Are you all
right?" His eyes were searching hers.

"Yes, of course. I'm fine." Or as fine as a seven-month-
pregnant woman with an active kicking person inside her
abdomen, a back ache and varicose veins could possibly be.

What did he want? She hesitated, wondering if she should
invite him in because at any moment Melinda and her four-
year-old and her parrot might be showing up. But she couldn't
just say, "Go away." She didn't want him to go away.

"Come in," she said and opened the door wider.

George came in. He didn't sit down. He paced around
her small living room even though she gestured toward the
couch.

"Won't you sit down? Would you like something to drink?"

He cracked his knuckles and shook his head. "Why didn't you say something?" he demanded, his gaze on her belly again.

Instinctively Sophy put her hands on her abdomen, as if they were a shield. She shrugged. "Say what? 'Oh, by the way, before he died, Ari knocked me up?' Why? What point was there?"

"He's responsible."

"Yes, well, perhaps he was. Now he's not. And he didn't want to be, anyway." She turned her back and fiddled with the blinds, but she heard something that sounded like George's teeth coming together.

"How do you know?" he demanded.

"I talked to him about it. I told him. He said, 'Oh, too bad. What're you going to do about it?'"

George muttered something and rubbed his hand against the back of his neck.

Sophy, watching him, tilted her head. "How did you find out?" she wanted to know.

"Your letter."

"Letter?"

"You wrote him. Told him. It was in his backpack. We found it when they finally shipped his stuff home."

"Oh. That letter." The one she'd sent when she'd first found out. The letter that Ari claimed he'd never got. "It was in his backpack? I see."

So Ari had already known about the baby before she'd tracked him down in person to tell him the news. When she'd never heard from him, she'd been afraid he hadn't received her letter. Obviously he had. He'd simply chosen to ignore the fact.

Somehow Sophy supposed she wasn't surprised. Not anymore. Not about Ari. Hiding his head in the sand and pretending it didn't exist was typical of Ari. Not surprising at all.

But finding George on her doorstep *was* surprising. What did he want?

Her back was hurting, so Sophy sat down.

George didn't. He was still prowling around her small living room, stopping only to stare down at the cradle and the stacks of tiny newborn clothes inside it that several of her coworkers had recently handed down to her. "When's the baby due?" he asked.

"Early October."

He turned his gaze on her. "And how are you going to cope when it comes?"

"What do you mean?"

"Who's going to take care of it? Do you have benefits? Can you afford to stay home with it?"

Sophy pressed her lips together, wondering what business it was of his. "I can manage," she said.

His hooded gaze bored into her. "Can you?"

His eyes were intense, magnetic. She couldn't look away. And at the same time she couldn't lie. "I hope so," she said more truthfully.

He came to stand directly in front of her so that she had to tip her head up to look at him. "We can help. We will help."

Sophy stared up at him. "We? Who's we?"

"The family." He paused. "Not just the family. Me."

"You?" She shook her head. "Financially, you mean? That's very kind. Thank you, but—" She should stand, should face him head-on.

"Financially, yes, of course," George cut in. "Your child will be taken care of." He said that almost impatiently. "Not just your child." He held out his hands to her.

Instinctively, Sophy put hers in them and despite her bulk and imbalance, in George's hands she felt herself pulled easily to her feet.

He didn't step back, so that now they were standing mere inches apart, close enough that Sophy could see that he'd recently shaved, that he had the tiniest chip out of one front tooth, that there were gold flecks in his intense green eyes.

"What then?" she asked.

"Marry me."

Her obstetrician had said, "Don't get up too fast. It can make you dizzy and unbalanced." He'd never said it would affect her hearing. Sophy stared, disbelieving.

"Marry me." George said it again. Urgently. His eyes mesmerized her.

Sophy swallowed hard. There was blood pounding in her ears. "I—I need to sit down," she said faintly—and sank into the chair before she tumbled into it.

"Are you all right?" George demanded. Then, "You're not all right." He crouched down in front of her so she was staring again into his beautiful eyes.

"I'm f-fine. Just—" Dazed? Confused? But he'd said it twice. She couldn't have misheard. Still, even sitting down, she couldn't make sense of it. Her mind reeled. "You don't mean that," she said finally.

"I'm not in the habit of proposing marriage if I don't mean it," George said stiffly.

"No, I didn't mean that. I meant—why?" It was almost a wail. She couldn't help it.

"Why? Because it makes sense. You're alone. You're having a child—my cousin's child. He can't marry you now—"

"He didn't want to marry me anyway."

George gave a dismissive wave of his hand. "I do. I can." So saying, he dropped into a crouch next to her chair and took her hand again, looking at her earnestly, intently. "I can, Sophy," he repeated in a low tone that spoke more to her than all his words combined.

Sophy could see in his eyes that he was serious. She studied his gaze, trying to make sense of what he was suggesting. It was outrageous, ridiculous. And terribly, terribly tempting.

She didn't know George. He didn't love her. He barely even knew her, so he couldn't possibly love her. And she didn't love him.

But she *could,* a tiny voice inside her spoke up. *She could love him.*

And heaven help her, she listened.

Maybe it was that her hormones had gone crazy during her pregnancy. Maybe it was how lonely she had been feeling lately. Maybe it was not wanting to raise her baby alone. Maybe it was how intently George was looking at her, how warm and strong his fingers felt as they wrapped around hers.

There were countless reasons. All sane and sensible and logical—reasons that, as he crouched beside her, George spelled out for her.

But Sophy knew that the tipping point had already happened. It had been his tone of voice when he'd said, "I can, Sophy."

His tone made her believe not just that he could, but that he wanted to.

Call her weak, call her foolish, call her naive. Call her hopelessly hopeful. All of the above.

"I don't know," she faltered.

His fingers squeezed hers. "You do know, Sophy," he said in that same tone. "Say yes."

She said yes. Holding hard to George's strong hard hand, she took a chance—on love. She leapt with eyes closed and heart wide open.

Yes. Take me. Take us. Love us. And let us love you in return.

They had married two weeks later. The ceremony was in the judge's chambers. Obviously not a big wedding. There was a small reception after at his parents' house. Mostly family. Mostly his.

Of hers only Natalie's mother, Laura, had been able to come. It hadn't mattered to Sophy. She was happy to have George's family become her family.

When she said her vows, she meant them. And when she looked up into George's grave handsome face and thought of spending her life with him, it didn't feel wrong. It felt right.

Almost like a dream come true.

Of course it wasn't. And Sophy knew better than to expect that.

But she could try to make it come true. She was going to make him so happy, be the perfect wife. And then maybe... Well, a girl could dream, couldn't she?

After the wedding George had moved into her place because it was near her work. He never said how far it was from his, but the distance didn't seem to bother him. George really never said much about his work at all. And whenever Sophy had asked about it, his replies were vague.

She took the hint and never pressed, not even when, at his parents' late summer party, his father happened to mention the job George would have at the University of Uppsala.

"Uppsala?" Sophy had echoed. She hadn't wanted to say, "Where's that?" So she looked it up when she got home. It turned out Uppsala was in Sweden.

Sweden. Yet he'd never mentioned it to her.

But then they'd only been married a month by that time. And theirs had hardly been a normal courtship and marriage. So if he hadn't mentioned it, maybe he'd just been too busy. And she'd been consumed with the last weeks of her pregnancy. Maybe he was saving it for after the baby was born when they could make plans.

It didn't matter. She didn't mind where they went. She'd always wanted to visit Sweden.

They did talk about a lot of other things—baseball, art, astronomy, food, music, movies, books—and the baby.

Because to her astonishment, in George Sophy finally found someone besides herself who cared about her baby.

At first she didn't talk about her pregnancy or the baby. She didn't think he'd want to know. Besides, she was terribly self-conscious about the way she looked as her body changed and her belly got bigger every day. A major turnoff, she'd have thought.

It wasn't as if he'd ever seen her naked before the baby. They had never been lovers. And the advanced stage of her pregnancy had precluded that happening any time soon.

Still she caught George's gaze studying her frequently, and he didn't seem put off by what he saw. Once when he was looking, the baby had visibly kicked and George's eyes had widened.

"Is the baby kicking?" he asked. "Does it hurt?"

And impulsively, Sophy had taken his hand and placed it on her belly to let him feel the baby's kicks. And watched his eyes widen even further, as if he felt something miraculous.

After that he began to ask questions. Then he began to read all her books on pregnancy and childbirth and asked even more questions—so many that she finally suggested, "Why don't you just come to my appointment with me?"

She'd been kidding, but he'd nodded. "Thanks, I will."

He'd attended the last few in the series of prenatal classes that she'd been attending. Sophy had been doubtful at first about his interest. But he'd never missed a class. He'd helped her with her exercises and practiced breathing with her. He even massaged her back when it ached and her feet when she'd stood on them too long.

And when she finally went into labor, he was right there with her, holding her hand, letting her strangle his, and when the nurse had put Lily in his arms, there had been a look on his face that had allowed Sophy to believe he loved Lily as much as she did, that everything would be all right.

Too good to be true?

In retrospect it felt like that.

Not at first, though. At first it had felt wonderful—or as wonderful as it could feel while Lily was colicky and fretful, Sophy was despairing of ever being able to cope and George, though working long hours, was there when she needed him, made her laugh, gave her the support she needed.

One night she was so exhausted, had no milk left, and Lily didn't want to nurse anyway. Sophy was at her wit's end when George said, "Let me take her. You get some sleep."

She hadn't wanted to be a bother to him, hadn't wanted to make his life difficult, but bursting into tears, which was the other alternative, wouldn't improve matters. She handed colicky Lily to George.

He snugged her against his bare chest, bent his head and kissed the top of hers lightly. "Come on, Lil, ol' girl. Let's go for a walk."

"Oh, but—" Sophy began.

"Just around the apartment," George assured her. "I'm hardly dressed to take her out." He was wearing pajama bottoms, nothing else.

Sophy knew he wasn't going anywhere. She just felt so helpless, and so perilously close to tears as Lily wailed on.

"Go to sleep," George said. "She'll be fine. I'll give her a bottle if I have to."

"But—"

"You've expressed milk. I know how to warm a bottle. Sleep, Soph. Sleep."

He carried Lily out of the room, crooning to her. Sophy watched them go, felt a stray tear slip down her cheek, felt like a failure. Knew she would not sleep.

She listened to Lily's wails disappearing as George carried her out of the room, then sank back into the pillows, miserable.

Turning onto her side, she drew George's pillow against her and buried her face into it to breathe deeply of the scent of him that lingered. And against all odds, she slept.

When she woke up it was to silence. No baby crying. No sound of George's light breathing from the other side of the bed. No George at all.

Lily wasn't in her cradle, either. A glance at the clock told Sophy that she'd slept two hours—a lifetime in the night of a fretful baby. She threw back the light cover and went to look for them.

They hadn't gone far. She found them in the living room. George was sprawled in the recliner, his hair tousled, his lips slightly parted, sound asleep. And Lily, fretful no longer, was lying on his bare chest with both of George's arms wrapped securely around her, fast asleep as well.

Sophy just stood there and stared, awed and in love—deeply in love—with both of them.

They might not have started out the way most families did, but that didn't mean they couldn't have a happy ending. She loved him, after all. And she began to think George loved her, too. But until the night before Lily's baptism, she hadn't really dared to believe it was true.

That night, shortly after Lily's two-month birthday—only a day after the doctor told her they could "resume marital relations"—George and she made love.

She had felt hot and cold and a little panicky at the doctor's assurance that making love would be fine. Physically, of course, she was sure it would be. Emotionally she hadn't been nearly as sanguine. What George thought, she didn't know. He never said. He would talk at length about planets, stars and the immutable laws of nature as well as about baseball and art and Lily, but he didn't talk about feelings at all.

There was no talk, only actions. It started simply enough—with concern and gentleness. A soothing back rub like many he had given her that soon became neither soothing nor confined to her back. His hands ventured further that night. They played in her hair at the nape of her neck. They traced the curve of her ear. They ran down her sides and over the swell of her buttocks.

They made her squirm with longing. She wanted more. She wanted him.

And as she turned and touched him, it was clear he wanted her, too. She knew, of course, after Ari, what a man wanted. But as in every other way, George was unlike Ari in the way he made love. Certainly he wanted what Ari wanted in one respect. But his lovemaking wasn't all about that. He gave as much as he took. And he let Sophy give as well.

It began slowly, but the fire soon burned hot. George's kisses, formerly gentle, now grew hungry and urgent, his touch compelling. His hands moved over her body, learning her secrets, sharing his own with her. When her legs parted and he slid between them, she knew a sense of rightness. And when he braced himself above her and began to move, she met him eagerly, drew him in.

And when they shattered in each other's arms, Sophy knew a sense of completion that she'd never felt before. At that moment she'd understood how two separate beings could become one.

She and George were one. She believed it.

Clutching him to her, then running her hands over his sweat-slick back, she shut her eyes tightly against the tears of joy she felt. But she couldn't quell them and they spilled onto her cheeks. She knew George tasted them when he kissed her.

He didn't speak, just pulled back enough to look down at her.

She opened her eyes and saw the expression on his face. "I'm sorry," she said. "I just—" But how could she explain?

George touched her cheek gently, then rolled off onto his back and lay beside her silently. Finally he said, "It's all right."

He turned toward her and stroked her hair lightly. "It will be all right. Lily will be awake before we know it. Let's get some sleep while we still can." Then he spooned his body around hers and said no more.

It will be all right. It already *was* all right. More than all right, Sophy thought as she had hugged the words to her heart in the same way she had hugged George's arm against her breasts.

But it hadn't been.

The castle of love and happily ever after that she'd dared to believe in that night had crumbled the very next day.

Now nearly four years later, Sophy knew she was in danger again.

All those old feelings were welling up. She had a soft spot for George. He was gorgeous, charming, brilliant and responsible. Everything a woman would desire.

He'd stepped in and helped her when she most needed his help. He'd married her and allowed her to fall in love with him and to believe he might actually love her, too.

It hadn't been true.

She needed to remember that because discovering the truth had hurt too much the last time. And once was definitely enough.

She wasn't about to risk her heart again.

CHAPTER EIGHT

THE NEXT MORNING, she began building a wall.

Not a literal wall, of course. But a professional wall. All nice and neat and absolutely appropriate. He was the client, she was the "rented wife" for the next two weeks or so. And she was determined to make sure they both remembered that.

So she fixed his breakfast before he came downstairs, set a place for him at the bar in the kitchen and placed a folded copy of the morning's *Times* next to the place mat.

When he appeared, she was on the phone, which worked out well. She didn't have to make chitchat with him, didn't have to even acknowledge their encounter last night. She just gave him a wave and pointed to the kitchen and kept on talking.

When she got off the phone, she went into the kitchen to find him staring into the open oven where she'd left his meal to keep warm.

"What's this?" he demanded.

"Your breakfast," she said briskly. "I have a lot of work to do this morning. Fridays I do the billing and fill out all the payroll sheets. I'll be doing some laundry today, too. Changing sheets. Lily's coming tomorrow. She can sleep with me."

He straightened up. "There's a bedroom at the other end

of the hall from mine that Tallie's boys use when they're here."

She'd seen it, but she didn't want Lily up there when she was on the floor below. "She'll be fine with me."

George's jaw set. "Maybe you could let her decide."

Sophy gave him a bright smile. "I'll do that." No problem at all. She was quite confident Lily would rather be with her rather than in a strange room in a house she wasn't familiar with. "Where's the laundry you need washed?"

He gave her a hard look that told her he knew exactly what she was doing, but he told her where the laundry was and then he limped past her to head for the stairs to his office.

"What about your breakfast?" she said.

"Not hungry."

She didn't talk to him the rest of the morning. She vacuumed and dusted and did the breakfast dishes, dumping out the food he didn't eat and muttering under her breath as she did so. The washing machine and dryer were at the other end of the floor on which he had his office, and when she went past, she could see him in there working at the computer.

She didn't stop and ask how he was feeling or make any comments at all because that would have undermined her intent to remain professional. George didn't look her way, either—which suited her fine.

She made his lunch at twelve-thirty and did go downstairs then to tell him it was ready.

He said, "What are we having?"

"You're having a ham sandwich and some coleslaw. I've already eaten." She folded her arms across her chest.

He tipped back in his chair and regarded her from beneath hooded lids. "What did you have?"

She felt a flush rise to her cheeks. "A sandwich."

"Ham?"

She pressed her lips together and made an affirmative sound.

He raised a brow. "And a little coleslaw?"

"I'm going to be busy," she said sharply. "We don't have to share meals!"

"I'm not paying you enough to share meals with me?"

"Damn it, George! Stop twisting things into meaning what they don't."

"Is that what I'm doing?" he said mildly. He shoved himself to his feet and started toward the stairs.

Sophy, who was standing between him and them, stepped quickly back into the doorway of the laundry room to give him room to pass.

He paused when he reached her, so close he nearly touched her. But he didn't. He just looked down at her. "Is it that distasteful, Sophy?"

She shook her head quickly. "No, of course not. I just—"

"You don't have to explain." His voice was curiously flat, and he turned and started up the stairs.

Sophy didn't go after him and when she came upstairs fifteen minutes later with a basket of folded laundry, the plate was empty, the sandwich was gone and so was George.

She felt an unwelcome stab of worry. She checked in the living room, but he wasn't there. Neither was Gunnar. Surely he hadn't taken the dog for a walk? He was moving better, but he still wasn't fit. Annoyed, she checked the back garden. He could have taken Gunnar down the steps from the small TV room behind the living room. He hadn't. She checked out the front door, too, scanning the entire block for any sign of him.

But he'd obviously got enough of a head start that she didn't see him at all. Damn him! How was she supposed to keep an eye on him if he didn't tell her where he was going?

She was still fuming when the phone rang. It was Natalie giving her details about their flight tomorrow, then asking how things were.

"Just peachy," Sophy muttered.

"George acting up?"

"George is gone."

"Gone? I thought he hurt his ankle. I thought he had concussion. I thought you were supposed to be watching him."

"Yes, well—" Sophy hunched her shoulders, feeling guilty "—I was putting laundry in downstairs, and when I got up, he wasn't here."

"You'd better find him then," Natalie said. "Lily is dying to see him."

"Lily doesn't even know him," Sophy protested, though she certainly knew lots about him. "It's Gunnar she'll want to take home with us."

"She's looking forward to seeing Gunnar, too," Natalie said. "And you," she added diplomatically.

"Thanks," Sophy said drily.

Natalie laughed. "That goes without saying. She's missed you tons. It's good she's coming. Now go find George so he's there when we get there."

"I'll be at the airport to meet you."

"Not necessary," Natalie said.

"Yes, it is," Sophy countered firmly. "I need to prepare Lily."

Natalie hesitated, as if she might argue, but then simply replied, "Suit yourself."

When they hung up, George still hadn't returned. Two hours—and more trips to the door to peer out looking for him than Sophy wanted to admit—and he still wasn't there.

She was seriously annoyed now. What did he think he was trying to prove? Just because she'd tried to put them on a business footing, he didn't have to walk out. She was still supposed to be looking after him!

She didn't know what to do. She could hardly call Sam and say she'd lost his patient. And she refused to call Tallie and ask if George had gone to see her. The last thing she wanted to do was upset his sister in the last weeks of her pregnancy.

She remembered how every little molehill had become Mount Everest when she was due to have Lily. She could just imagine what thoughts of a missing brother with a head injury might induce.

She started dinner because the pulled pork she was fixing had to cook several hours. Once it was in the Crock-Pot, she made herself focus on the weekly billing work she had to do for Rent-a-Wife.

Once every bit of billing and electronic filing had been done, she went back into the kitchen, began to shred the pork, and then made Lily's favorite chocolate oatmeal cookies, partly because she knew her daughter would be delighted, but mostly to give herself something to do while she gnashed her teeth and muttered out loud about George.

She washed the kitchen floor, folded the laundry, then, still muttering, hoisted the full laundry basket into her arms and trudged upstairs. She put all her things away, then carried George's laundry up to his room. She could put the clean sheets on his bed while she was here.

Or she could have if George himself hadn't been sprawled facedown, fast asleep on the mattress pad.

Sophy stopped dead in the doorway, staring in disbelief.

He was *here?* He'd been here the whole afternoon?

She sucked in a sharp breath. Gunnar, lying beside George with his head resting on George's back, lifted it to look at her and thump his tail once or twice.

The movement of the dog or the sound of her indrawn breath woke George up. He made a groaning, waking sound and she saw him flex his shoulders, then open his eyes. Catching sight of her in the doorway, he rolled over.

"I'm sorry," she said hastily. "I didn't know you were here. I—I thought you'd gone out."

"Wished?" George asked, his voice still rough with sleep. He didn't get up, but folded his arms under his head and looked up at her.

Sophy shook her head. "No," she said truthfully before she could decide if that was a good idea or not. But she was so relieved to see him she couldn't have dissembled if she'd tried.

"Good." There was just a quiet satisfaction in his tone that touched her somewhere deep within. "Are we eating dinner together?"

"I didn't want to presume," she began.

"We're eating dinner together," he decided firmly. He pulled an arm out from behind his head and rubbed his belly in anticipation as he sighed. "It smells great. I'm starving."

"You had a sandwich—"

"I gave it to Gunnar."

They ate dinner together while Sophy kept the conversation on neutral impersonal topics—the weather, the Yankees' chances to win another pennant, the reviews of a new Broadway play.

George let her. It was enough, he told himself, to share a meal and savor both the food and the conversation.

But of course, it wasn't.

Not even close. He wanted it all.

But he'd jumped the gun four years ago, had manipulated Sophy into a marriage she hadn't really wanted. And he wasn't going to do it again. She deserved better. So did he. He had learned his lesson.

Or, damn it, he was trying to.

But it was difficult. Beyond difficult. Next to impossible to sit there and discuss the Yankees—or worse, a play he had no intention of seeing—when he didn't give a damn about either of them. Only about her.

Patience, he advised himself. At least they were sharing a meal, even if they weren't, at the moment, sharing a bed.

It wasn't just the lack of sharing a bed that bothered him. It was being shut out of her life, being told by her actions as well as her words, that he didn't matter, that she didn't love him.

Because he loved her.

Love. Whatever that was.

He wasn't used to dealing in love. He didn't understand it. He was a scientist, damn it. He dealt in natural laws and forces. Love was not one of those.

And that was why he was grinding his teeth and answering her questions about the Yankees' pitching rotation—because loving her meant letting her make her own decisions. It ought to have been easier. He was a scientist, after all. He was used to setting up experiments and then keeping his hands off, stepping back to observe the results, not provoke them.

But he was a man, too—a man who knew what he wanted and went after it. Which he'd done last time, he reminded himself. And look how that had turned out.

So he resolutely sat through another twenty minutes of talking about the Yankees before he asked, "Do you want to take Lily to a baseball game?"

Sophy blinked, her fork halfway to her mouth. "Lily? To a baseball game? Why would I want to do that?"

George shrugged. "You seem very gung ho," he pointed out. "I thought maybe you'd instilled some of that enthusiasm in Lily, too."

"Not yet," Sophy said. "She's a little young."

"What does she like?"

For a moment George thought she would brush off the question. It was more personal than anything she'd been willing to talk about so far this evening. But then she smiled and got a faraway look in her eyes. "She likes the beach and swimming. She likes books. She loves being read to. She likes going to the park and playing on the swings. She likes dogs," she said, glancing down beside the table where Gunnar lay sleeping. "She'll like Gunnar."

"He'll like her, too," George said. "What time will she be here?"

"I'm going to meet them at the airport about three tomorrow afternoon."

"I'll come with you."

"You don't need to do that."

"I want to," he said before he could stop himself. Ah, well. A man could only stand by and watch and wait for so long. Besides, it was the truth.

Sophy looked mutinous, but he didn't back down. Instead he finished the last of his pulled pork, then stood up and carried his plate to the sink. "Great dinner," he said. "Thanks."

"You're welcome. It's what I'm here for," she said brightly.

George knew that.

But, heaven help him, he was still hoping for a whole lot more.

"Are you sure you wouldn't rather stay home?" Sophy said the next afternoon. She was heading out to get into the hired car for the journey to the airport and, true to his word, George was right behind her. "There's really no sense in your getting worn out."

"It'll be good for me," he said cheerfully.

He wasn't using the crutches today, and he moved much more easily, though he was still wearing the boot. Still, when he'd come downstairs this morning she had seen increased agility in his movements. He didn't act as if every move hurt, either.

She was torn between being glad he was recovering and wishing for something that would keep him home so she could spell out the ground rules to Lily.

"It's really not necessary." She made one last-ditch attempt to dissuade him as he held the door to the car open for her. "You should rest. You've been working all morning."

He had gone down to his office after breakfast—one she'd prepared, like yesterday, after she'd already eaten her own. George had scowled at her when she said she'd already eaten. But at least he'd eaten it this time.

Now he slid in beside her, shut the door and waited until the car service driver pulled away from the curb to say, "I had some stuff to get done so I could come. I did it. And if I need to rest, I can do it right here. Put my head on your shoulder?" he suggested with a smile.

The words and the smile sent a wave of something that might have been desire washing right over her. Her cheeks burned, but she made herself shrug and say, "Of course. But I must warn you, I have very bony shoulders."

The way he looked at them induced an even stronger surge of desire. But he only smiled as if he were considering the option for a moment before he settled back against the seat. So she didn't get his head on her shoulder. But that didn't stop her being intensely aware of him as he lounged easily beside her in the confined space. It was a long drive out to JFK. She found herself wishing Natalie had chosen to fly into LaGuardia.

"Nonstop flight to JFK," Natalie had explained when she'd called. "I figured it was better with Lily."

No doubt it was. But it wasn't better with George.

"You mustn't let Lily bother you," she said to him now. If she couldn't lay down rules for Lily, she'd have to do it with George. "I'll try to keep her out of your way."

"Why?"

"Why?" She stared at him. "Because she's four years old and she's still learning when not to interrupt. Trying to work around her is not easy."

"We'll manage," George said confidently.

Sophy wasn't quite so confident. "Just don't yell at her."

George's eyes widened. "When did I ever yell?"

"Well, you didn't. But she was a baby then. I'm only saying." Sophy shifted farther away from him, feeling awkward.

George rested his arm along the back of the seat. His fingers were perilously close to her shoulder. "You don't have to worry," he assured her. "I like kids. I know how to deal with them."

Sophy supposed that was true. He had nephews, after all. And it was certainly true that he had a devoted friend in the little boy down the street. Just this morning while George was in the shower, Jeremy had knocked on the front door to see if his friend George was there and ask if he could come out and play.

"Not yet," Sophy had said, biting back a smile. "He's supposed to take it easy awhile longer."

Jeremy's mother, who had come with him, apologized for disturbing them. "I told Jeremy it was too soon, but he wanted to check. We all feel terrible that George got hurt. He saved Jeremy's life. If there's anything we can do for him—"

Sophy shook her head. "He was happy to be there." She knew that, however badly George had been hurt, that was certainly true.

He was, ever and always, responsible. Throwing himself in front of a truck was just another example of his determination to do whatever needed to be done.

And how could you argue with it? How could you say he shouldn't do it?

You couldn't.

All you could do was feel petty and ungrateful when he did it for you—which was exactly how Sophy felt. She turned away and stared out the window, trying to figure out how to explain him to Lily when she would have bare minutes to do so. She still didn't have any good plan by the time they arrived at the airport.

Fortunately their timing was good and as they were ap-

proaching the terminal, she had a call on her mobile phone
from Natalie saying that they had landed.

"Terrific," Sophy said. "I'll meet you at the baggage claim
and George will wait with the driver."

"George?" Sophy could hear the surprise in Natalie's
voice.

"Yes," she said and hung up. "It's too long a walk for you,"
she told him. "You didn't bring your crutches."

She didn't wait to hear any discussion. The minute the
driver pulled up to the curb, she was out of the car and strid-
ing quickly toward the automatic doors. It took her only a few
minutes to find the right luggage area and spy Natalie and
Lily waiting for their bags.

"There you are!" she called, and at the sound of her voice,
Lily turned, spotted her and came running.

"Mommy!" The little girl launched herself into Sophy's
arms and wrapped small arms around her mother's neck in a
fierce hug. "It was a long, long plane ride. I was good. Well,
pretty good. Mostly good."

Sophy buried her face in her daughter's dark curls and
breathed in the scent of fresh shampoo and warm child. Dear
God, how she'd missed her baby.

"Mostly good, hmm?" she murmured. She gave Lily a mul-
titude of small kisses, then glanced up inquiringly at Natalie,
who grinned in response and gave her a thumbs-up.

"She was mostly super," her cousin confirmed, keeping
an eye out for the bags as she answered Sophy's question.
"Sometimes a little impatient. But she's just been eager to get
here. Ah, good. Here they come."

She grabbed a weekender bag off the luggage carousel.
"I didn't need much because I'm going home tomorrow. But
Lily, well—" Natalie shrugged and laughed as she wrestled
another much larger bag onto the floor "—Lily thought she
should come prepared."

Sophy gaped at the huge bag. "Where did you get that?"

"It was Christo's. He used it when he was a kid and flew back and forth between his mother in California and his dad in Brazil. He said he kept his life in this suitcase."

"An' now it's mine. Christo said I could have it," Lily told her eagerly, "so I could bring everything I need. An' I did. I brought my books and my bear and my dolls and my building set and—"

"Good heavens," Sophy murmured, looking askance at Natalie, who gave a helpless shrug.

"I didn't figure George had toys," Natalie offered.

"And some clothes," Lily went on. "An' I brought Chloe 'cause she wants to meet Gunnar." Now she craned her neck and looked around eagerly. "Where is he?"

"He's waiting back at the house. We couldn't bring him to the airport," Sophy told her daughter.

Lily's lower lip jutted. "Why not?"

Before Sophy could answer, a voice came from behind her. "Because she brought me instead."

She spun around.

George was right behind her, his gaze intent—and not directed at her at all. He was looking at Lily.

"I thought you were going to wait in the car."

"No."

"I said you didn't need—" she started to protest, but George cut her off.

"Yes," he said firmly. "I did."

There was an urgency in his tone that made her look at him more closely. His eyes held a glitter of green fire as he added, "I wanted to."

And in his voice she heard it again—the same urgent note, even though he was speaking quietly, his words almost getting lost in the vast noisy room full of people.

"I've waited a long time for this," he said, his gaze meeting hers for a long moment before returning to focus on her daughter. "I wasn't waiting any longer." Then his gaze softened and the corners of his mouth tipped up in a smile. "Hello, Lily."

In the circle of her arms, Sophy felt her daughter stiffen at the sound of her name. Her eyes first narrowed with curiosity, then widened as she regarded him with a certain dawning awareness. "Daddy?"

The look on George's face was all the answer she needed.

Suddenly the little girl began squirming so determinedly that Sophy nearly dropped her. "Lily!"

But Lily wasn't listening. She flung out her arms to George and cried, "Daddy!"

Daddy.

George felt his throat close. And it had nothing—physically, at least—to do with his daughter's stranglehold on his neck. He nearly stumbled as he caught her midleap from Sophy's arms. But he steadied himself and drew her close as Lily's little arms nearly choked him. She gave him a smacking kiss and wriggled closer still in his embrace.

"Ah, Lil." He buried his face in her hair and simply breathed her in. He'd had her in his life such a short time that, after she was gone, he'd told himself he couldn't possibly miss her that much.

It wasn't true. He'd missed them both. He'd felt an emptiness inside him every single day.

"Daddy," Lily was saying, pulling back away enough so that she could look up into his face and pat both his cheeks. She was grinning at him, claiming him.

George was happy to be claimed. He grinned back, his throat still too tight to begin to form words. So he reached up and stroked a hand through her hair, marveling at it. There was so much of it now, a curly glossy thick dark brown that had only been hinted at in the baby-fine hair she'd had the last time he'd held her and kissed the top of her head.

He leaned in and kissed it again now, savored its silky softness against his lips, then found himself blinking rapidly against suddenly watery eyes. He cleared his throat, too, and was relieved to find the constriction had eased, that he could probably talk without his voice breaking like a kid's.

He secured Lily in one arm and held out a hand to Sophy's cousin. "Hi. I'm George. You're Natalie? Thanks for coming." He smiled at her as he gave Lily a squeeze. "Thanks for bringing my girl."

And yes, his voice almost did break on those last two words, but at least he got them out.

Sophy's cousin smiled, too, taking his hand and looking at him with a mixture of avid curiosity and frank assessment. "Yes, I'm Natalie. I'm glad to meet you. At last." There was a wealth of speculation in those added words. He supposed he didn't blame her for them. He didn't know what she knew, what Sophy had told her.

He'd avoided looking at Sophy since Lily had thrown herself into his arms. He'd heard her gasp as Lily's leap had unbalanced the two of them, and her exhalation of relief when he caught Lily and steadied them both. But he didn't want to see whatever raw emotion had been on her face at that moment.

He was too afraid he knew what it would be.

Now he slanted a glance her way. "Do you want to take her while I take her bag?" he offered.

She looked as if she would very much like that, but after a moment's hesitation, she shook her head. "The bag is cumbersome. With your foot, it wouldn't be easy for you. I'll manage it, if you'll take care of Lily."

"You sure?" He was surprised and grateful, guessing how much it cost her. "Really, I can handle it." He nodded again at the bag.

But Sophy shook her head and allowed him a fleeting smile, though her gaze slid away from his almost as soon as it connected. "No. Go ahead. I'm sure."

"Can I ride on your shoulders?" Lily asked him.

Wordlessly, George swung her up onto them, trying not to wince at his muscles' protest.

"Lily, he's been hurt," Sophy admonished her.

"It's all right," George said quickly. Not painful at all compared to what losing her had been like.

But Lily wasn't convinced. She leaned down and tilted her head so she could look him in the eye from about two inches away. "You're hurt?" She sounded worried and she stroked his hair as if she were comforting him.

"I'm fine," George said. "I'm especially fine now," he assured her, leaning nearer to kiss the tip of her nose, "because you're here."

Sophy watched them go.

She didn't even breathe, just stood and stared as George strode off—doing his best not to limp, she noted—with Lily perched on his broad shoulders as comfortably as if she did it every day of the week, her fingers fisted in his hair.

It had to hurt. But George said no.

As Sophy watched, George glanced up at Lily and said something. Sophy saw his teeth flash white in a grin. And Lily gave a little bounce and nodded her head vigorously, then patted George's hair.

"Well, she certainly has him wrapped around her little finger." Natalie came to stand beside her, but her gaze—like Sophy's—was on the two who were almost at the sliding doors.

"Looks like," Sophy agreed, trying not to sound as disconcerted as she was feeling. She hefted Lily's gargantuan bag and began to lug it after them.

"You'll kill yourself doing that," Natalie objected. "You take one handle and I'll take the other." She grabbed one away from Sophy and looped it over her shoulder, then started forward, towing the weekender bag with her other hand. So Sophy did the same with the other handle and kept pace.

"He's nice," Natalie decided after a moment. "I like him."

"You just met him," Sophy said irritably. "Besides, I never said he's not nice."

"You said he broke your heart."

Sophy wished she hadn't. There was such a thing as too much honesty. Now she said, "I was just trying to warn you about Savas men. Warn you off Christo."

"Lot of good that did," Natalie said cheerfully.

Sophy grunted.

"Don't be grumpy," Natalie said. "It worked out all right in the end, didn't it?"

"For you it did. But—"

"Exactly. For us it did," Natalie agreed. "And maybe it will for you, too."

"When did you change your name to Pollyanna?"

Natalie just laughed and shook her head, then nodded toward the two figures on the other side of the glass. They'd reached the car and George had swung her down to the ground. Immediately Lily fastened her arms around his leg and hung on. "She likes him," Natalie pointed out.

"She was supposed to like Gunnar," Sophy said plaintively as they reached the sliding doors which opened for them and they lugged the bag through it.

"She will," Natalie said at once. Then her expression turned to one of commiseration. "I think she might like both of them, Soph."

"Yeah." That's what Sophy was afraid of, too.

If Sophy was a bundle of contradictions, her daughter was an open book.

Lily knew what she liked—and didn't like—and she said so. She liked the beach and the ocean and tall buildings.

"Like that one," she said, pointing up at the one they were passing on their way back to his place. "An' that one." She jabbed her finger in the direction of another. "An' I like to read stories an' I like chocolate ice cream. But I don't like butterscotch." She turned in his lap so she could show him the horrible face she made.

George laughed and made a horrible face right back at her. She giggled and bumped her forehead against his chin.

"Lily, sit still," Sophy said sharply.

George nearly said, "It's all right," because he had a grip on her and she wasn't going to get hurt. But he didn't want Lily to get the idea she could pit one of them against the other. So he said quietly, "Turn around. Look over there. Do you like horses?" he asked as the car came along Central Park South and a line of carriages and horses stood waiting to take tourists for a ride.

Lily turned, following the way he pointed, and bobbed her head eagerly, pointing, too. "Look, Mommy! Horses! Can we go for a ride? Please?"

George didn't know how Sophy would answer that, and he didn't wait to find out. "We can," he said preemptively. "But not today. You've had a big day already today. We'll go one day next week."

"What day?" Lily asked. "Monday? Can we go Monday?" She looked at him avidly.

Out of the corner of his eye, George saw Sophy bite back a smile. In response he felt one creeping onto his own lips, knowing he'd asked for that one.

"Wednesday," he told Lily. "Promise," he added and held his hand out in front of her to make it official, wondering if four-year-old girls even knew how to shake.

This one did. She even gave a firm nod of her head. Then she said, "How many days until Wednesday?"

Sophy smothered a laugh.

Hearing it, George couldn't help grinning, too. "It's Sat-

urday afternoon," he told Lily. "Then Sunday." He ticked it
off on his fingers. "Then Monday." Another finger.

"An' Tuesday," she said. "An' Wednesday." She counted
up on her fingers, too, then looked at the total in dismay and
turned sad eyes on him. "Four days is a long time."

"Not that long," George assured her. "You'll have other
things to do as well."

"Like what?" Lily and her mother and even Natalie, who
was up front with the driver, all looked at him with interest.

Obviously generalities wouldn't work. He tried to think
what little girls liked to do. Trouble was, he had no idea. He'd
played with his brothers. He only had nephews so far. And
his one sister, Tallie, wasn't any help at all. She had always
played cops and robbers like "one of the boys" or fashioned
herself as "chairwoman of the board," when playing make
believe on her own.

"Well, obviously playing with Gunnar," he said because he
knew Lily wanted to do that. "And walking Gunnar. Taking
Gunnar to the park. He's really looking forward to meeting
you," George added, sure that Gunnar wouldn't mind a little
prevarication in the aid of a good cause. "And it won't be
long now," he added as their car passed the Natural History
Museum heading up Central Park West.

Apparently Gunnar was distraction enough. Lily bounced
forward on his knee, looking out the window eagerly. "How
much farther is it?" she wanted to know. "How old is he? Do
you think he'll like Chloe, too? Can we take him for a walk
as soon as we get there?"

The questions spilled out far faster than George could
answer them. But he tried. And all the while he could see
Sophy next to him, torn between shushing Lily and enjoying
the spectacle of his having to deal with a four-year-old.

Let her smile.

She didn't have any idea how glad he was to have to deal

with this particular four-year-old, how much he'd missed her—and her mother—these past four years, or how very badly he wanted them back in his life forever.

CHAPTER NINE

IT WOULDN'T LAST, Sophy assured herself.

Yes, George was being kind now. He was answering Lily's endless questions with remarkable patience, allowing himself to be clambered upon and clung to, and generally tolerating far more childish behavior than any man should have to endure. More than tolerating, he really seemed to enjoy it.

But this was the first day. The first few hours, in fact. And it was a weekend, as well.

It wouldn't last.

George was a busy man, a physicist who was far more at home in the lab than in the playroom. He would soon tire of a four-year-old's chatter and want to get back to meaningful work. He had certainly worked long hours when they'd been together four years ago. She knew from the work she'd seen him doing on the computer that he was working just as hard now.

And though he'd been there to help her in the first months of Lily's life, he hadn't done it because he wanted to.

He'd done it because he'd felt obligated.

Obligated, Sophy forced herself to repeat in her mind now as she looked out the window down to where George was showing Lily how to throw a ball for Gunnar in the back garden. He'd felt obligated.

But there was no need for him to feel obligated any longer. George didn't owe them anything. He never had.

She needed to make sure he remembered that. So that when he lost patience, he didn't need to feel bad. She would just have to make sure he didn't hurt Lily in the process.

"He's a lot more kid-friendly than I imagined," Natalie said, coming to stand beside her and watch George, Lily and Gunnar in the garden. She held a coffee mug to her lips and sipped from it as she watched.

"Early days yet," Sophy replied.

Natalie raised her brows. "You think?"

"Of course."

"Seems to me like they get along fine."

"Yes. But as I said, early days. She's only been here a few hours."

Natalie shrugged. "Maybe you're right."

"I am right," Sophy said in an uncompromising tone.

Natalie laughed. "Famous last words." She glanced at Sophy and added, "But you haven't been here just a few hours."

Sophy felt something like a frisson of danger on the back of her neck. "What do you mean?"

"I've got eyes. And it doesn't look to me like it's business as usual with George. I've seen you working. I know."

Sophy shrugged. "So we have a history. It's over."

Natalie laughed. "Sure it is. That's why you watch him when he's not looking."

"He's been hurt," Sophy said defensively. "I have to make sure he's all right. I have to make sure Lily doesn't inadvertently hurt him more."

"Of course you do." Natalie dismissed that excuse with a wave of her hand. "And that's why he watches you the same way. Hungrily. And that's not in the past, not by a long shot." She paused and then slanted a glance in her cousin's direction. "Wouldn't you like it to work, Soph?"

The question cut far too close to the bone. Instinctively Sophy turned away from it.

"I'm not a dreamer," she said sharply. "I'm a realist. We married for the wrong reasons and maybe he does *want* me, but that's not the same as loving me. Sex is easy for men."

Not for her. She couldn't separate her emotions from the act. It was why she hadn't slept with anyone since…since George, that one night four years ago.

Natalie stared at her, eyes wide, wordless.

And in the face of her cousin's astonishment, Sophy hugged her arms across her breasts and plunged on. "What I would really like," she said fiercely, "is for him not to be quite so charming because when we leave, I do not want Lily to be hurt!"

Natalie's eyes got even wider, but she still didn't say a word.

Of course she didn't, Sophy thought disgustedly. What could you say in the face of a completely unexpected outburst? Damn it. She wanted to crawl into a hole. Why had she shot her mouth off? Why had she acted as if she cared?

Why *did* she care?

The realization that she did pulled her up short. Stopped her dead.

Wouldn't you like it to work?

Casual innocent words. Words that she'd blithely believed would come true once upon a time four years ago.

And when it hadn't, she'd turned her back. She'd had to turn her back. She'd had to make a life for herself and her daughter. She'd had to refuse to hope.

And now hope—a tiny tempting flicker of hope—stirred to life deep inside her.

It made her question her sanity, to tell the truth. Surely she couldn't be contemplating the possibility of life with George again…

Could she?

No. She couldn't!

But…

But she found her gaze once more drawn to the garden where George and Lily were laughing together. It was pure, unaffected laughter between two people totally in tune with each other.

Father and daughter.

No.

Lily was Ari's daughter.

But George was the only father she'd ever known. Not that she remembered him, Sophy reminded herself. But George was the one Lily asked about when she talked about her daddy. George was the one whose picture she kept alongside one of her mother on her dresser. George was the one she had recognized instinctively at the airport, the one she hadn't let go of since they'd arrived.

And he seemed to feel the same way.

Early days, Sophy cautioned herself, distrusting it all, doing her best to kill the flicker of hope.

It didn't make sense. None at all.

Why, given what she knew about why George had married her, was she fool enough to wish?

Of course it was true what Natalie said, on a physical level George probably did want her. Once he had. Once she had wanted him, too. To be honest, she still did.

But so what? She wanted more than that. She wanted love. To love. To *be loved.*

Not to be a duty. Not to be "one of Ari's messes" that George felt obliged to clean up. The very words she'd heard him say the day of Lily's christening. The day when her world collapsed.

George hadn't said it to her. He hadn't said anything much to her. She thought it was his way to do, not say, and she was fine with that.

But at Lily's christening, she'd come to fetch them for the

family pictures and what she'd heard him say to his father had changed everything.

They had been arguing, voices raised. Socrates was a notorious shouter, but she'd never heard George raise his voice until that day. She could still remember the exact words of their conversation as if they were emblazoned on her brain.

It was George's voice she'd heard first as she'd approached the closed door. He was insisting loudly that he didn't want to do something—something that Socrates was just as loudly demanding that he should.

She had been just about to knock, to call them for the family pictures and also to defuse whatever their argument was about, when George said, and she would remember his words forever, "I'm tired of cleaning up Ari's messes, damn it! Give me one good reason why I should?"

Sophy felt as if she'd been punched. She stopped dead outside George's father's office door, unable to breathe, only able to listen.

So she heard Socrates's one good reason. Actually he provided several—all very rational. "Because you're good at it," he'd said. "You don't take things personally. You don't overreact. You do what needs to be done and you never get emotionally involved."

Sophy's mouth went dry. Her heart was hammering so loudly she was surprised they didn't think there was someone knocking at the door.

But they didn't hear her at all. They simply continued, oblivious.

"Well, I don't want to," George said, sounding as quietly rational as his father expected now. "I have other things to do."

He didn't elaborate. Socrates didn't ask.

It struck Sophy that Socrates didn't care. He only cared about cleaning up the loose ends of Ari's life—"Ari's messes." And George was clearly the man he wanted to do it.

"It won't take long. It's hardly a big obligation," Socrates had said. Then he'd continued persuasively, eventually promising that this would be the last time.

"The last time?" George had said doubtfully.

"Well, he's dead, isn't he?" Socrates sounded exasperated. "What more trouble can he make?"

George hadn't answered that. He'd only said grimly, "It damned well better be. Because after this, I'm finished. I've got a life, damn it. Or did you forget that?"

"Of course I didn't," Socrates said indignantly.

"At least you can't expect me to marry this one," George said.

The words were like a knife through her heart.

But as she stood there, Sophy knew them for the truth. He'd married her to satisfy the family's expectations.

It all made a certain horrible sense. That job in Uppsala that George had been supposed to get, the job he hadn't bothered to mention to her—she knew now why he hadn't bothered. It was a part of his life that he'd put on hold because of her. He hadn't mentioned it because he wasn't going to take it—because Ari had died leaving her alone and pregnant.

Needy. *A mess.*

One that marrying her would clean up. For the family, For her. For Lily.

He'd as much as said so when he'd asked her to marry him.

He'd said they would take care of her. They! His family. Not him. She understood then that he had been simply doing what was expected because he was "the unemotional one," the one who didn't take things personally, who came in and did the dirty work when it needed to be done.

He'd never loved her.

She'd only hoped.

She'd believed his actions spoke for him, that by marrying her he was showing how much he did care. And the night before Lily's christening, when they'd made love for the first time, she dared to believe then that he more than cared—that he loved her the way she'd grown to love him.

That night had been magic to her.

But the next afternoon, she discovered how very wrong she'd been. Worse, she had realized that she was standing in the way of George's real life, that he'd married her to "do the right thing," and that she had to do the right thing in turn.

She had to stand on her own two feet, end their marriage and send him away. Set him free. Obligation free.

So she had.

She hadn't done it calmly or rationally or with any of that unemotional detachment that allowed George to do difficult things. No. She'd just turned on him, had told him to get out, that their marriage had been a mistake, that she wanted him gone!

He'd looked at her, astonished, as if he couldn't believe his ears. Then he'd argued a little, had told her she needed "to see reason."

But reason was the last thing Sophy had wanted to see then!

"Go away! We're through." Not that they'd ever really begun. She'd been adamant through her tears.

And in the face of them, George had gone.

He had quietly disappeared from her life as efficiently as he'd appeared in it, leaving her empty, hollow, more shattered even than she'd ever felt in her life.

But she'd pulled herself together and coped. She'd crossed the country and made a new life for herself and her daughter. She was a strong, self-reliant woman who didn't need a man to make her whole.

She and Lily were not obligations, or duties, or, God help her, a mess to be cleaned up.

Did George understand that now?

Did they have a chance this time? Was Natalie right? Was there more to their relationship than even Natalie saw?

Sometimes over the past week, Sophy had thought so. But she'd been afraid to trust. She still was. But was turning her back the coward's way out?

Did she wish their marriage would work?

God, yes. In her heart of hearts, unacknowledged to anyone, even her cousin and best friend, Sophy knew she still wanted it all.

Now, standing next to Natalie, looking down into the garden where George hunkered on the grass with his arm around Lily, their two dark heads bent together as he talked to her, Sophy felt her heart squeeze tight with love.

Yes, she loved him. Still. Yes, she wanted him. Always. Yes, she wanted forever with him.

But did she have the courage to risk gain?

George wasn't sure when he started to hope.

Maybe he'd never stopped. Certainly he'd never got the divorce and he'd never felt the urge to make a commitment to another woman. Hell, he'd never got beyond a few casual dinners.

But he knew exactly when he started to believe they might make it again as a couple—as a family.

It was when they'd seen Natalie off the next morning in a cab to the airport.

They'd stood waving on Central Park West until she was out of sight. And then it was just the three of them.

For a moment it seemed as if there was no sound in all of Manhattan—as if everything stopped. And then Lily had grasped one of his hands and one of Sophy's and then she'd swung between them, beamed up at them and gave a little skip. "Let's go home," she'd said.

And when George's gaze had met Sophy's over Lily's head, she had smiled at him.

Smiled. A real smile. Not a polite one. Not a strained one. Not a defensive one.

It was a little tremulous, perhaps. Even a bit tentative, he admitted, because George believed in accurate assessment of evidence. But it was a smile. It was something to build on.

And George wanted to build.

He met her gaze, held it. Then he offered her a smile, too. "Let's go home."

It was the most amazing thing, but Sophy felt as if she were being courted.

She'd never really been "courted" in her life. She'd had dates with boys and she'd been taken for a ride by Ari and she'd been married in a rush and cared for by George.

But until now she'd never really been courted.

She told herself it was silly to feel that way. But something about George's attentiveness awoke the feeling and she couldn't quite shake it.

Not that she wanted to.

She liked to cook and she would have happily made dinner that night listening to the sounds of Lily and George talking in the living room. But it was so much more enjoyable to have them appear in the doorway as she was peeling the potatoes and hear George say, "What can we do to help?"

She tried to tell them she was fine on her own. But they didn't leave. George showed Lily how to peel carrots, and then he chopped them into pieces for Sophy to add to the potatoes and meat in the stew she was making.

They prepared the food together and then, while it was cooking, George suggested they take Gunnar for a walk in Central Park.

Lily was already running to the door. But Sophy had to say, "Are you sure? You've been on your ankle a lot today. And what about your head?"

"My head doesn't hurt at the moment and the ankle isn't

bad. I won't overdo it. Promise." He flashed her a grin that was half-hopeful, half-conspiratorial and altogether too appealing. "Come on, Sophy. Don't be a spoilsport. How often do we get such a perfect day?"

And so she went. She wouldn't be a spoilsport. And he was right about the perfect day.

It was a bright sunny crisp autumn afternoon and the leaves were turning gorgeous shades of red and gold. Lily, unused to seasonal changes, was thrilled with the "painted leaves." She loved scuffing her feet through the piles on the ground, then picking up armfuls of them, twirling around and tossing them over her head.

"You should choose a few good ones," George told her, "and you can make stained glass window pictures."

"With leaves? Window pictures? How?" But Lily stopped spinning and began hunting leaves with George.

"We want whole ones," he told her. "As perfect as you can find them. And the brightest colors. My mother used to do this with me and my brothers and sister every year. Don't you want to help?" he said to Sophy when she stood back watching them, not wanting to intrude.

And so she began looking, too. They ended up crawling around on the ground, sorting through the leaves, picking and choosing, saving the best of the best.

"This can't be good for your ankle," Sophy protested once.

But George just shook his head. "Some things are more important than my ankle." His gaze left hers, found Lily, and then after a moment of just watching his daughter crouched down in silent consideration of which was the better of two leaves, it came back to Sophy again as if to say, "See?"

"You're right," she said. "They are."

Eventually they had collected a dozen brilliantly colored leaves, which Sophy was pressed into transporting as carefully as possible while George held Gunnar on the leash and carried Lily on his shoulders as they walked back home again.

There, while Sophy watched, George taught Lily how to make the leaves into "stained glass" window pictures by laying them between two sheets of waxed paper, then spreading one of his old T-shirts over them and ironing them with a warm iron.

"Not too hot," he explained. "We just want the wax from the two layers to melt together with the leaves inside. Here." He lifted Lily up onto a chair and helped her lay the iron on them, then smooth it back and forth.

Sophy opened her mouth to tell him to be careful, to say that Lily was barely four, that she could get burned. But then she shut her mouth again because George was being careful. He was helping Lily do it herself, but at the same time making sure she didn't get burned.

When at last Lily had pressed them to George's satisfaction, he took the iron and set it over on the counter where she couldn't accidentally touch it. Then he removed the T-shirt and held the rectangle of waxed paper up against the window.

The late afternoon sun shone through it, lighting up the leaves, making them gleam like stained glass against the windowpane.

Lily clapped her heads. "'S beautiful," she said. "Look at the red. An' the gold. Let's do another."

They had leaves enough left to do several more. So she did another. Then George started one. But after he'd put down two leaves, he looked over at Sophy. "Don't just stand there," he said. "Help me. I have no artistic skill whatsoever."

It was patently not true. He knew what he was doing, but she appreciated the invitation. She stepped up to the ironing board to help. George handed her the leaves. Their fingers brushed.

It meant nothing.

Nothing! Sophy assured herself. Yet hers seemed to tingle

after the barest touch. Surreptitiously she rubbed the tips on the side of her jeans, as if that would mask the feeling. It did nothing except make her fumble one of the leaves and tear it as she tried to lay it on the paper.

"Oh! I'm making a mess of this."

"No, you're not. It's only torn. Nothing's missing. Besides, it's easily mended." He took the leaf and laid it flat. Then with careful capable fingers, he pressed the tear together and laid the second piece of waxed paper on top of it, then flattened it down. Sophy took the T-shirt and spread it over them. Then, because he made no move toward the iron, she reached over and picked it up.

With the iron she pressed firmly down on the shirt, moving it slowly, rubbing it back and forth as George had done, then finally lifting it away. "Enough?"

Wordlessly George picked up the shirt and lifted the waxed papered leaves, holding them up to the light so the sun shone through them. "Beautiful," he echoed Lily. Then he pointed to the leaf that had been torn.

"See? It's fine. All better," he said as Lily examined it closely. "Good as new."

It was, Sophy thought, looking at it, too. You couldn't even see the tear. Torn and then mended.

Like her heart?

She didn't know, but it felt that way as the days passed and they grew together as a family…

On Monday George had to go up to the lab. He had grad students to work with and a project of his own he was working on. "Come with me?" he suggested that morning.

"Is your head bothering you?" Sophy asked immediately.

He hadn't complained at all over the weekend. But he'd gone to bed early Sunday night—actually at the same time Lily did, which pleased the little girl no end. And it was much easier to get her to go to bed with the assurance that Daddy was going to bed, too, and would be sleeping right down the hall.

He'd assured Sophy he was just tired, which she had readily believed. But now she wondered if he just hadn't said.

"It's not bad. Kind of a dull ache. Nothing like before. But," he added with a grin, "if it will get you to come, I'll bang it on something and make it hurt worse."

Sophy couldn't help laughing. "Don't you dare."

So she and Lily rode the metro train up the Hudson with George, and while he was working in the lab, they wandered around the streets of the local village, played a bit in a small local park and met George for lunch at a diner overlooking the river.

"Bored?" he asked. "If you want to take an earlier train back to the city, you can certainly do it. I didn't think I'd be tied up this long."

"We're fine," Sophy assured him. "We've had a good time exploring. We went in some antiques shops and a toy store and there's a small local museum."

"Give me another hour then?" George said. "And I'll be ready. Come and get me at the lab."

He finished his lunch quickly and strode away toward the lab. Sophy and Lily dawdled, watching a sailboat on the river and telling stories about where it might have been.

"I like sailboats." Lily said. "Daddy says Uncle Theo has a boat. D'you think I can go on it? Can you an' me an' Daddy go sailing sometimes?"

"I—well…maybe," Sophy said. Could they? Would they? A week ago she would have said it was impossible. Now, like the marines said, perhaps the impossible might happen. It only took a little longer.

When the hour was up, they walked up the hill to where the lab—which was really in a large house on a sprawling Hudson River acreage—was. George was sitting on the steps waiting for them. He had his briefcase beside him. But in his hands he had something else bright blue and red and yellow and green which he finished putting together as they approached.

He stood up, grinning, the breeze tousling his hair, as he held it out toward Lily

Her eyes widened. "It's a kite!"

It was indeed. And George told Sophy he had bought it at the toy store they'd visited earlier. He'd stopped in on his way back to the lab after lunch.

"I thought since you've been so patient, we might give it a whirl," he said to Lily. "Have you ever flown a kite?"

She shook her head slowly, eyes still wide. "But I seed 'em. At the beach. And I wanted to."

"Now's your chance," he said. "Just wait a minute while I put your mother's together."

"Mine?" Sophy blinked.

"More fun with two," George said. "We can share. Okay?"

"Yes," Sophy said, more delighted than she wanted to admit.

George put the kite together quickly, then tied tails on each of them and attached the balls of string. "Here's the rub," he said ruefully to Sophy. "After I had this great idea and bought the kites, I realized I can't run worth a damn. In fact I can't run at all. So—" he held out the ball of string "—if I hold it here, can you move out a ways and give it a pull? Run a bit if necessary?" His grin was abashed, but his eyes were twinkling.

And Sophy wondered how she was supposed to resist a man who made a kite for her?

She took the ball of string and backed away across the grass, playing the line out and keeping up the tension at the same time. Then he tossed the kite as she gave a jerk on the line and—

"There it goes!" cried Lily. "Lookit! Oh, lookit!" She pointed as the kite rose and dipped and then jerked on the line in her mother's hands. Sophy discovered she had to hang on tight or she would lose it.

"Are you sure about two of them?" she asked George, walking back toward him, trying to keep her eyes on the kite but finding them straying more often to the man.

"Let her hold that one," George said. "And we'll get this one up."

"It's pretty strong," Sophy said cautiously.

"She's a pretty strong girl, aren't you, Lil?" George asked his daughter.

Lily held out her hands and bobbed her head. "I can do it, Mommy," she said. "Please?"

So Sophy passed over the ball and George looped it around Lily's wrist so she wouldn't lose it, then placed it in her hands, showing her how to play out the string or pull it back if she needed to.

"How will I know?" Lily asked, her expression serious. Her tongue caught between her teeth.

"You just try," George told her. "You do the best you can. You feel the way the wind pulls it and you trust your instincts."

Sophy hoped that was good advice—to trust her instincts. Not just about kites but about life, because heaven help her, she was trusting hers.

Lily loved the kite flying. They all did. It was a fabulous day. And Lily protested when Sophy called a halt to it because she saw lines of strain around George's mouth.

"It's all right," he said.

"It was," she agreed, even as she brought her own kite down. "It was lovely. But we're not going to overdo it."

She thought he was going to argue with her.

"We can do it again another day," she said quickly.

The mutinous look in his eyes faded instantly and he gave her a brilliant smile. "You're right."

She could tell his head was hurting by the time they got

back home. So she left Lily to take care of him while she took Gunnar out for a quick walk and picked up a pizza to bring home for supper.

When she got back it was nearly dusk and George was lying on the sofa with his eyes shut. Lily sat beside him stroking his hair. She looked up when Sophy appeared. "I'm the nurse," she told her mother. "Daddy says this makes him feel better."

"That's very kind of you," Sophy said gravely. "Now wash your hands and come and eat. Do you want any pizza, George?"

Wincing he sat up. "Yeah. Sure." He got to his feet and started toward the kitchen. The pain in his face was obvious.

"Bed, I think," Sophy said firmly.

"I'm all right. I can eat—"

"If you want pizza, I'll bring it to you. Go up and go to bed. You overdid it. You need to lie down."

"But I told Lily—"

"Lily wants to take care of you. She'll understand that taking care of can mean letting someone sleep to get well. Now go." She pointed toward the stairs.

It was evidence of exactly how much his head must really have been hurting that George didn't object further.

He went.

He slept like the dead all night. Sophy knew because she got up to check on him several times and, in fact, spent the night in the room where Lily was sleeping right down the hall so she could be nearby if he needed anything.

He didn't. And in the morning, while he was a little wan looking, he seemed none the worse for wear. He even took Lily and Gunnar to the park while Sophy got breakfast.

"Are you sure about this? You were pretty exhausted last night," she reminded him.

"We'll be fine," he said. "Besides, I have Lily to take care of me."

The little girl beamed.

Tallie called the next afternoon to see how George was. She was delighted to learn that Lily was there.

"The boys will want her to come over," she said. "They want to meet their cousin. Can she come over Thursday afternoon and stay for dinner? I'd invite you and George, too," Tallie went on frankly, "but I thought you two might like some time on your own, yes?"

Sophy swallowed, feeling slightly light-headed at the thought. She understood the wealth of meaning in Tallie's invitation and in the suggestion that she and George spend time together. She knew, too, that with each step she was getting in deeper. But knowing, while it made her breathless, didn't make her able to resist.

She didn't even want to resist.

She wetted her lips. "That sounds like fun," she said. "Lily would love that."

Lily was, as expected, thrilled at the notion. She had made friends with Jeremy already. And having her very own friend right down the street to play with while George was at work and Sophy needed to get things done online and on the phone, was wonderful.

But the idea of cousins was even better. She'd never met a cousin before—except Natalie who was a grown-up and didn't count. She could hardly wait until Thursday afternoon when she and Sophy would take the subway to Brooklyn and she could meet them.

And when Sophy's phone rang midmorning, she said to Sophy, "Maybe that's them, telling us to come early!"

"I doubt it," Sophy said with an indulgent smile, then answering the ring.

"It's Tallie," her sister-in-law began. "I have a favor to ask."

"Sure, name it." Sophy prepared herself to console Lily when Tallie explained that it wouldn't work out today.

"Could you and Lily come now? And stay? Take care of the boys, I mean," she said apologetically. "I know it isn't what we planned, but I'm afraid I'm having the baby!"

CHAPTER TEN

"YOU CAN BE MY Rent-a-Mom," Tallie told Sophy cheerfully as she kissed her boys and gave them last-minute instructions while Elias tried to chivy her out the door.

"You don't have to rent me," Sophy replied "I'm glad to do it. Just go now—and have a safe quick delivery and a healthy baby girl."

"I will," Tallie promised, giving each boy another hug. And then she gave Lily a hug as well. "I hope she's just as beautiful as this little one."

"Come on. Come on," Elias muttered, Tallie's overnight case in one hand and his wife's arm in the other. "You don't want to have this kid in the entry hall."

Tallie just laughed as Elias steered her out the door toward the waiting cab. "He's always like this," she said. "A basket case."

"Damn right," Elias said, "and I have reason. Digger was almost born in the cab. I'll call you," he told Sophy. "Mind," he said sternly to his sons.

The three of them bobbed their heads solemnly. "We will."

And surprisingly, they did. The twins took Lily off to show her their toys and she went happily. The little boy, a three-year-old named Jonathan, but called Digger, stayed with Sophy and looked worried.

"Everything will be fine," she assured him. "Would you like to read a story?"

He nodded soberly and went to find not one but twenty books, which he brought to her.

"Are all these your favorites?" she asked as she settled him on her lap and opened the first of the books.

He gave another nod. Sophy began to read. By the fifth or sixth book, Digger began to tell her about the pictures and which characters were the best. By the tenth, he was telling the story along with her. And by the last one, he was taking her by the hand and saying, "Wanna see my trucks?"

She accompanied him out to the small back garden where he showed her his trucks in the large sand box where deep holes and tunnels provided evidence as to how he got his nickname. "Did you do all this?" Sophy asked him.

Digger nodded happily, and there was a real light in his eyes. "Me 'n' Uncle George."

"George—I mean, Uncle George dug this with you?"

"Uncle George likes to dig. Sometimes we go to the beach an' dig. We make plans. Wanna see our plans?"

"I'd love to." Sophy followed him back into the house and into the family room, where he tugged out the bottom drawer of a large map cabinet.

"Here." He pulled out papers that held simplified diagrams and elevations of a series of tunnels and pits.

Sophy stared at them, amazed and captivated. The drawings were neat and meticulous—exactly the sort of work George did when he was designing an experiment—but on a basic elementary level.

"You don't just dig a tunnel," she murmured, tracing one of the passages with her finger.

"You can," Digger told her. "Sometimes we do. But sometimes they fall in. So we plan. It works better. When's my mommy coming home?"

Ah. For all that Digger was happy to show her his things, his mother was never far from his mind. "Probably the day after tomorrow," Sophy told him. "She has to have the baby and then have a day or so to rest. It's a lot of work having a baby," she told him.

"Daddy says I was in a hurry," he told her. "Maybe the baby will be in a hurry, too, an' she can come home sooner."

Sophy brushed a hand over his glossy dark hair. "Maybe she will."

But they had no word the rest of the afternoon, so apparently the new baby wasn't in as big a hurry as Digger had been. By the time George got there at five, Elias still hadn't called.

"He hasn't?" George scowled, looking worried.

Sophy stepped between him and the boys so they couldn't see the expression on his face. "Not yet. But I'm sure he will before long. Babies come in their own good time," she said cheerfully to the boys.

"Ours didn't," George muttered under his breath.

Sophy remembered Lily's birth all too well. Her labor had been long and painful and twice had seemed almost to stop before a sudden rapid delivery that had made her strangle George's hands.

"That was my first," she said quietly just to him and then more loudly so the boys could hear. "I'm sure Tallie is an old hand."

"Can we call her?" Nick asked.

"Or Dad?" Garrett suggested.

"I think they're pretty busy right now," Sophy said. "Your dad will call as soon as something happens."

"Come on," George said briskly. "Let's go over to the park and play ball."

Sophy went along and played, too, determined to make

sure that George didn't overdo things. But she needn't have worried. Lily took care of that.

"My daddy gets a headache when he plays too long," she told the boys. "So we can only play for a little while."

"How come you get a headache, Uncle George?" Garrett wanted to know.

So George explained about the incident with Jeremy and the truck. The boys were all wide-eyed with awe and appreciation. And Lily clearly basked in his reflected glory.

"Daddy's a hero," she told them solemnly.

George shook his head. "A guy's gotta do what a guy's gotta do." Then, "Come on, let's play ball."

They played. And Sophy, watching, thought that however good a father George was with Lily, she could easily imagine him with sons as well. Lily brought out his protective instincts as well as his playfulness. But with the boys there was a different sort of rapport and a rugged role model that they could emulate.

She stood there, smiling, as the sun went down, turning the red and yellow leaves to copper and gold. When her phone rang, she plucked it out of her pocket.

It was Elias. "It's a girl. She and Tallie are fine." His voice quavered a little. And Sophy heard him take a deep breath. "It was an emergency C-section in the end. The cord was around her head."

"Oh, Elias!"

"She was cutting off her own oxygen. And Tallie was a wreck. I was, too," he admitted. "But—" another breath "—she's okay now. Everyone's okay."

"Wonderful," Sophy breathed a sigh of relief, too. "I'm so happy for you. Here. You can tell the boys."

She called them over and let them each talk to their father while she told George and Lily the news.

"We can go see 'em after we eat dinner," Nick reported, beaming. "Dad says so."

And Digger's eyes shone when he handed the phone back to Sophy. "Let's go eat dinner."

Alethea Helena Antonides was a lot smaller than her name. But with big eyes, round cheeks, rosebud mouth and a thick cap of fine dark hair, she was absolutely beautiful.

When they got to the hospital, she was snug in Tallie's arms, having just nursed. Her brothers all peered at her, wide-eyed, then looked at their mother as if they were still not sure what had happened or what was going to happen next. Tallie looked exhausted but radiant. Elias just looked beat.

"She's gorgeous," Sophy breathed.

And George, holding Lily up so she could get a better look at her newest cousin, nodded and swallowed as he studied his niece. "Very nice."

"Just nice?" Tallie looked indignant.

"*Very* nice, I said," George corrected her. Then he swallowed again, looking at his sister. "She's beautiful, kid. I'm glad you're both okay."

Tallie reached out a hand to him and he gave hers a squeeze.

"Me, too," Lily said and wiggled her hand in between theirs. "I like your baby," she told Tallie. Then she looked around at her own mother. "Can we have one, too?"

Sophy felt her cheeks suddenly begin to burn. She didn't dare look in George's direction. "Here, Digger," she said, hoisting the little boy in her arms. "I bet you'd like to come sit up here by your mommy and Thea."

Digger liked that very much. Then all the boys crowded on the bed with their mother and sister and father, and George took their picture. Lily wanted to be in it, too.

"No, honey. That's *their* family," Sophy said as George snapped a couple more.

"Then Uncle Elias can take one of *our* family," Lily insisted. "Me an' you and Daddy."

Sophy looked at George. George looked at her. Lily looked at both of them, then took matters into her own hands. "Here." She grasped them each by the hand and pulled them to the chair. "Daddy, sit here."

Obediently George sat. Then without waiting for further direction, he hoisted Lily up on the arm of the chair, then tugged Sophy down onto his lap.

"George!" she protested as she bounced onto his thighs. But he simply wrapped a strong arm around her and tugged her back hard against him. And Sophy had no will or desire to protest. She could feel his breath against the back of her neck. It made her knees weak.

"Smile," Elias commanded and snapped the picture. He studied the image. "Not bad." He took another and another. "Yeah," he smiled at the last one. "That'll do."

Each of the boys then got to have their picture taken with their new sister. And Elias took one of Lily holding Thea, too, because he said, "You girls have to stick together."

Picture taking done, it was time to take the children home.

"Could you guys stay the night?" Elias asked as they were leaving. Under his elation he looked ragged and strained, his cheeks stubbled, his hair uncombed, his shirttails hanging loose. "I hate to ask you. I know you've been there all day. But—" he shook his head wearily "—I want to stay here. I *need* to stay here tonight." He glanced back across the room at Tallie, who was holding Thea again. And there was such tender longing in his gaze that Sophy touched his arm.

She understood his words. Understood his need. Thea's birth had been difficult and scary. No one said so, but all the adults knew it could have had a very different outcome. "Of course," she said. "I'll stay. George will have to see to Gunnar, but—"

"I'll go home and put him out, then I'll be back," George said. "You stay with Tallie."

Elias gave them a grateful smile. "Thanks. I'll be home to take Nick and Garrett to school. And I'll bring Digger back here with me."

"Take as long as you need," Sophy told him. "We'll be fine."

She took the kids home in a taxi while George caught the subway back to the Upper West Side. She oversaw baths and snacks and was letting the twins read in their beds while she read to Lily and Digger when George returned bringing a backpack with a change of clothes for her and Lily. His were in his briefcase, he told her. And he had to leave early to go home and put Gunnar out again before he headed up to the lab for a meeting with some high-powered grant people early the next morning.

"I'm afraid I'm sticking you with a lot," he said. "I'd change it if I could. But it's a meeting we've had on the books for weeks."

"Not a problem," Sophy assured him. "Why don't you read to the kids while I clean up the kitchen?" It was in the same state they'd left it when they'd gone to the hospital right after they'd eaten.

"I could clean up the kitchen if you'd rather," George offered.

Sophy shook her head. "You read. Lily likes it when you read to her. You do the best growly voices," she quoted their daughter with a smile.

George smiled, too, a slow and, to Sophy's eyes, sexy smile that curled her toes. "A man's gotta use his talents," he said in his best growly voice. Then he winked and headed upstairs.

Sophy rinsed the dishes and put them in the dishwasher, then turned it on and wiped off the table and countertops. She didn't get to hear the growly voices because George was up in their bedrooms. When she finished, she climbed the stairs, but it was quiet.

One peek in the back bedroom showed her that Digger and Lily were already fast asleep. Nick, too, was sprawled fast asleep in the top bunk of the room he and Garrett shared. Garrett still had his nose in a book. She didn't see George.

Then she heard a noise and turned to see him coming out of the bedroom at the front of the house, carrying a pile of laundry in his arms.

"I changed the sheets in Tallie and Elias's room," he said.

And that was when Sophy realized there was only one bed.

The look on her face must have betrayed her realization. George's expression didn't really change so much as his eyes seemed to shutter for an instant before he said, "You don't have to share it, Sophy. Not if you don't want to."

But even as he said the words, Sophy knew she did.

"I do," she said, meeting his hooded gaze and feeling rather as if she were making a vow. "If you do."

A muscle in George's jaw ticked and a corner of his mouth lifted. "Oh, yeah."

She gave him a tremulous smile and reached out to take the sheets from him. Their fingers brushed. "I'll just take these downstairs and turn off the lights."

George was waiting when she got back. He had turned down the bed and left on only the single small reading lamp by the bed. "Do you want a shower?" he asked.

She nodded, then made a face. "I feel like I'm covered with peanut butter and jelly and mac and cheese."

He grinned. "A little boy's delight." But the look he gave her, though hungry, was far from boyish. He raised his brows. "Want me to wash your back?"

Sophy wet her lips nervously. "That would be...lovely."

Their eyes met and Sophy felt the awareness tingle all the way to her toes.

And it was. He took his time undressing her, peeling her sweater over her head, then stopping to kiss her neck before proceeding. She fumbled with the buttons of his shirt and felt like an idiot when he did them for her.

"Sorry," she mumbled.

"I'm just impatient," he said, a rough tremor in his voice. "It's been a long time."

Never, in fact. They had never taken a shower together. He had never washed her back. And by the time they were undressed, it wasn't clear that they were going to take one together this time, either—or if their desire would lead them straight to bed.

But just then George, kissing her cheek, murmured, "Mmm, grape, I think," and Sophy laughed.

"Yes, shower time for sure," she decided, and stepped in. Fortunately George had already turned it on, so the water was warm. So was the slick wet body of the man who stepped in behind her, who reached around to cup her breasts and nibble his way along her shoulders.

"I thought you were going to wash my back," Sophy said, shivering with delight at the feel of his lips on her skin and at the press of his erection against her bottom. She leaned back into him, moved.

George groaned. "Getting there," he muttered and went right back to nibbling. But one hand did leave her breasts long enough to snag the soap. He skated it over her belly, then slowly and sensuously worked up a lather, which he spread over her breasts, along her ribs and around to her back.

But washing her back meant stepping away, leaving space between them. And just as she was about to object to that, George turned her in his arms and wrapped them around her, rubbing soapy hands over her back while his chest and her breasts got better acquainted. Then his hands dipped lower, slid between her legs.

Sophy's knees trembled. Her breath caught. She ran her hands up his abdomen, then caressed his chest, his flat belly, his sex.

A breath hissed out from between George's teeth. "Soph," he warned.

But Sophy was beyond warning. She was learning his body all over again. She touched her tongue to his nipples. She scraped her fingernails along his ribs. She smiled at the low growl of need and pleasure when she stroked him.

At that touch his whole body went rigid.

"George?"

"Just…getting a grip," he said through his teeth. His eyes were dark as midnight, glazed with desire.

"I could…get a grip," she murmured.

He gave a strangled half laugh. "Don't."

"No?"

He shook his head. "It will be better…this way." And he rinsed his hands, then grasped her ribs and lifted her.

Instinctively Sophy wrapped her legs around him and felt him fill her. Her breath caught.

"All right?" George held her, didn't move.

Sophy nodded, putting her arms around him, giving a little wiggle that made him bite his lip.

"Ah," he breathed. And then he began to move.

Sophy's nails bit into his shoulders. Her heels pressed against the backs of his thighs. And as they moved she felt the tension grow, the power surge between them, felt her body tighten and then shatter around George even as he came within her.

He sagged back against the shower wall, still holding her, wrapping her tight. And Sophy clung to him as she tried to find words to express what this meant to her. But the words were lost in the emotion. Her heart was too full. And when she tried, when she lifted her face to look at him, and saw him looking down at her, his gaze dark and intent, no words would come.

He stroked her face with the tips of his fingers, then touched his lips to hers. "Beautiful," he said.

Yes, just one word. She could live with that.

They washed all the soap off. They dried each other slowly and carefully. And then George took her to bed and they made love all over again.

Sophy said it now as she curled into George's side and rested her cheek against his chest. He was already asleep. But it didn't matter. She could tell him tomorrow. She could tell him every day for the rest of their lives.

She would, too.

George would have preferred to stay in bed with his wife.

His wife. The words made him smile.

When his watch alarm went off at five-thirty, he briefly debated calling up his colleagues and grad students and the grant from Washington and telling them so, then grinned as he imagined the dropped jaws and the sputtering that would greet any such announcement.

He turned his smile on Sophy, who slept curled against his side, her cheek resting on her hand. There had been no tears last night. No Ari, hovering like a specter, over their lovemaking. This time she was his—wholly and completely.

George bent his head and pressed a light but possessive kiss to her cheek. Then, because there was never any doubt about what he had to do, he levered himself quietly out of bed and headed to the bathroom.

He took a quick shower, trying not to let his mind linger on the memories of what had happened in this shower just scant hours before when he'd last stood under this spray—with Sophy in his arms.

But it wasn't easy, especially when the merest recollection

had him ready to go back to the bedroom, slide back into bed next to her and take things up all over again.

Deliberately he turned the water to cool, then cold. It helped, but not much.

He shaved, dressed and combed his hair, then went into the bedroom to put on his shoes. It was still quite dark and his eyes, unaccustomed to the dimness, didn't notice that Sophy was awake until she said sleepily, "Good morning."

He could hear the smile in her voice. George smiled, too, then finished tying his shoe and crossed the room to bend over the bed and kiss her. "Good morning yourself."

She shoved herself up on one elbow and looped her other arm around his neck, deepening the kiss, making him ache.

God, he wanted her. He glanced at his watch. It was still too dark to make out the time, But he knew he didn't have enough without even looking. Regretfully he pulled back from her embrace. "I have to go, Soph."

She sighed. "I know." She settled back against the pillow and he could feel her gaze on him as he tried to knot his tie in the dark. "Do you always do what you have to do, George?"

"What?" He threaded the end through the loop, then frowned. "Pretty much. Doesn't everyone?"

"Ari didn't."

Ari! Damn it to hell! Was it still Ari? Was it *always* going to be Ari?

"I'm *not* Ari," George said through his teeth.

"I know that."

"I'm not ever going to be Ari," he went on, jerking his tie tight, practically strangling himself.

"You married me because of Ari," she said quietly.

He sucked in a breath, wanting to deny it entirely but knowing that he owed her the truth. "Yeah, I did." He scrubbed a hand over his face. "And I'm sorry I did," he added harshly because God knew that was the truth, too. "I shouldn't have done it."

Sophy sucked in a sharp breath, but she didn't speak. She didn't move. She didn't say a word.

George ground his teeth, then glanced at his watch and could finally see the hands well enough to know there was absolutely no time to discuss and explain anything as important as this right now. He raked a hand through his hair, undoing everything the comb had accomplished minutes before.

Then he sighed and shook his head. "I'm sorry," he said again. "But we can make this work, Soph. But right now I have to get to this meeting...."

Sophy lifted a hand and gave it an almost dismissive wave. "Go," she said quietly. "By all means, just go."

CHAPTER ELEVEN

SOPHY DIDN'T TELL Elias they were leaving New York when she and Lily left the house that morning.

She just said goodbye to George's brother-in-law and told him what a wonderful family he had and how lucky he was to have them. And if she teared up a little saying it, well, the adults in the house were all a little emotional that morning.

Elias was still a bit rattled from his daughter's birth. He still looked tired, and he was clearly distracted, busily chivying the twins into the car to go to school and then putting Digger in his car seat so they could go from school directly back to the hospital to see Tallie and Thea. He didn't notice the quaver in her voice at all. He was simply very grateful she had stayed the night.

"We'll have you guys over when we're home and organized," he promised. "Tallie will want to say thanks. And the boys will want Lily to come over."

"Thank you," Sophy replied because it was all she needed to say. She and Lily saw them off, Sophy did up the breakfast dishes and then they took the subway back to George's.

"Where's Daddy?" Lily wanted to know. "Where did he go?"

"To the lab," Sophy said. "He had an early meeting."

"So we couldn't go with him," Lily said. "Maybe we could

go now?" she suggested brightly after a thoughtful moment's consideration. "We could take the kites."

"No," Sophy said. She had almost said, "Not today." But that wouldn't have been fair. That would have been misleading. "No," she repeated. "We have to go—" she almost said home, too, and stopped herself before she did "—back to the house and let out Gunnar." Then she took a deep breath and added, "And then we have to go home."

"Gunnar is home," Lily said, misunderstanding.

Which just made it that much harder. "No, to our home. With Natalie and Christo. In California."

Lily shook her head. "This is our home," she said. "With Daddy."

Sophy didn't argue. She tried another angle. "It's Daddy's home. And you can come stay sometimes—" because that was obviously necessary now "—but it's not my home. And I need to go home, Lily."

"But—" Lily might only be four, but she had mastered the art of argument.

Sophy tuned it out. She stared straight ahead and didn't listen, though doubtless everyone else in the subway car was. It was a blessed relief to get to their 86th St. stop and get off.

Gunnar was delighted to see them. Lily took him out in back and threw tennis balls for him, pointedly ignoring her mother since Sophy had ignored her arguments. It wasn't ideal, but it was better than the alternative, which was Lily kicking and screaming her way back to California.

Sophy stood in the living room, waiting for an airline ticket agent to take her call, simultaneously looking through the window down at Lily and Gunnar, and remembered the day George had been there with them. She remembered his arm around Lily, their two heads close together as he'd talked to her about the dog. It was then that she'd begun to let her defenses crack. She should have known better.

Well, now she did. She wiped a tear away just as the agent came on the line.

"I need two tickets to Los Angeles," Sophy said. "Yes, for today."

George was not distractable.

His single-mindedness was legendary, his preparation exemplary. He always focused on the object at hand. And he never ever, as his father was fond of saying, got emotionally involved. He was perennially practical and perpetually unperturbed.

Except today.

Today he had to fight to keep his concentration focused on the meeting taking place. He was thinking about Sophy. He had to struggle to remember the details that usually sprung from his lips at the slightest question. He was remembering their night together and the way she closed up on him this morning.

He said, "Sorry?" And "What?" and once he even said, "Huh?" which had his colleagues confused and his grad students befuddled and made the grantors scratch their heads and say they thought they'd like to come back and discuss the project another day.

"Good idea," George said briskly, grabbing at the possibility of an early departure. "Let's do that."

"Here's your hat, what's your hurry?" Karl VanOstrander, the senior physicist on the committee murmured.

"What?" George was already stuffing papers in his briefcase.

Karl just shook his head and clapped George on the shoulder. "Nice to see you're human," he said.

George didn't realize there had ever been any doubt. But he just nodded absently and headed off to the station at a brisk pace.

He tried calling Sophy's phone as soon as he was on the

train, wanting to know whether he should come back to Elias and Tallie's or go to his own place. He supposed he should stop at his place even if Sophy was still at Tallie's. Gunnar would need letting out.

She didn't answer, so he called Tallie and Elias's. No one answered there, either, which didn't precisely help him know where she was. She might even be at the hospital seeing Tallie and the baby.

He cracked his knuckles and punched in Sophy's number again.

In the end he decided to go back to his place. Gunnar would need out. And if Sophy wasn't there, he could always grab clean clothes for all of them and head back over to Brooklyn.

He bought a bouquet of daisy mums at the corner market on his way. It had never occurred to him, but these flowers reminded him of Sophy—they were fresh and bright, and just looking at them reminded him of the joy Sophy brought into his life.

Clutching them, he pounded up the steps to the brownstone. Gunnar was in the entry hall. Sophy and Lily weren't there.

Well, fine. He'd go over to Elias and Tallie's. If Tallie were home, she'd laugh at the sight of him with flowers. She might even think they were for her—and the baby. He'd buy her some if it made her happy, but these were for Sophy.

"Go on out," he told the dog, opening the door to the back garden. Then, while Gunnar was outside, he went up to get Sophy and Lily clean clothes.

The closets were bare.

George stared at them. Shook his head. Felt it begin to pound at the same time that his stomach turned over.

Get hit by a truck? It was nothing compared to getting hit by this.

She'd left him. Turned away from him. Again.

She couldn't do that, damn it! He'd let her do it once because he'd pushed her too fast, had wanted too much.

Now?

He kneaded the back of his neck, tried to ease the pain in
his head. Nothing at all would ease the pain in his heart.

Only Sophy's love could do that.

In her university days, Sophy had had one of those old posters
on her wall that proclaimed splashily, *Today is the first day
of the rest of your life.*

When she was in college that sort of thing had been inspir-
ing. It had urged her to look forward, to see endless possibilities, to forget about the past, the failures, the shortcomings.

Nice work if you can get it.

And Sophy had been able to when she was at university
because her past had been short, her failures relatively incon-
sequential and her shortcomings no big deal.

Now it was different. *She* was different.

Her past was long enough to include Ari and George
and consequent disasters. Her failures in these relationships
bordered on magnificent. Her shortcomings were obviously
substantial.

All that she saw in the future was misery and all that she
felt was pain.

And a stiff neck which came from spending much of the
night in Lily's bed with her daughter and Chloe to keep Lily
from crying on and off the whole night long.

It was what she'd done all day.

Sophy didn't blame her. The fault was hers. If it had been
necessary to bring Lily out to New York, she should have
made sure her daughter knew it was only temporary. Saying
so after the fact didn't have the same effect.

Lily just glared at her or said, "We didn't have to leave
without saying goodbye."

And Sophy could only shrug and say, "Yes, we did. I needed

to get back," when what she really meant was "*I* needed to leave." It was as simple as that.

And as selfish, she admitted. So she promised Lily that she could go back and spend time with her father soon. She didn't doubt that George really cared for the little girl. It would be good for both of them.

Lily didn't think that was much consolation. "I want Daddy," she'd sobbed when she went to bed last night. "I want Gunnar."

"You have Chloe, darling," Sophy assured her.

Lily had flung Chloe across the room, then bounded out of bed, grabbed her, then threw herself on the bed, clutching Chloe and sobbing harder.

"She'll get over it," Natalie had said earlier in the evening. "Kids are resilient."

She hadn't asked what happened. She'd just picked Sophy and Lily up at the airport and given them both hugs. Sophy had been grateful for the understanding and the lack of questions. All night long, listening to Lily's periodic sniffles, Sophy had hoped that Natalie was right.

Now she eased herself out of bed so as not to wake Lily, then flexed her shoulders and moved her neck. It hurt. Her eyes felt as if someone had thrown a pailful of sand into them.

"Today is the first day of the rest of my life," she said to herself as she padded into the bathroom.

It did not sound promising.

She took a long hot shower and refused to think about the shower with George. She washed her hair, then put on a clean summer-weight T-shirt and a pair of shorts. It might be fall in New York, but it was nearly always summer in California.

She put on the coffee and then booted up her computer. Work was solace. Or it should have been. But thinking about renting wives was too close to home. She shut off her computer and stared into space—not a good place to be.

The knock on the door was a welcome jolt out of her self-pitying misery. It was barely seven-thirty. Hardly time for visitors. But maybe Natalie had come to see how she was doing on the way to the office. Natalie, after all, had come back from Brazil in a similar state some months ago.

She raked her fingers through still-damp hair and hoped that Natalie wouldn't notice—or at least wouldn't comment on the dark circles under her bloodshot eyes. Then, pasting on her best "I'm doing fine" smile she opened the door.

"What the hell did you think you were doing?" George strode past her into the room and wheeled on her, eyes flashing.

Sophy, stunned, stared at him. This was the first day of the rest of her life, damn it. George was not supposed to be here!

But he was—and he looked as bad as she felt. His hair was tousled, his jaw was stubbled. His eyes were bloodshot, too. He looked strained and pained and angry as hell.

She'd never seen George angry. She didn't want to now.

"Go away," she said, still holding the door open, making a sweeping gesture toward it, hoping he would do just that.

He ignored her, walked in and flung himself on her sofa. "I'm not going anywhere." He looked up at her defiantly, then raised one dark brow. "Want to try to make me, Sophy?"

She ground her teeth, and shut the door, then set her hands on her hips. "I shouldn't have to," she told him. "I don't know what you're doing here. Well, I do know, but there's no reason."

He stared at her, then frown lines creased his forehead. "You know, but you don't think there's a reason?"

"No, I don't." She folded her arms across her chest and met his gaze with a steely one of her own.

For a minute he didn't say a word. She dared hope he would get up and walk out before she begged him to stay.

But then he said, "Why am I here?" in that quiet, measured

very George-like tone. That was the tone she recognized, the one completely at odds with the one he'd used when he'd burst in here.

She could deal with that one. So she made herself shrug negligently. "Because you always do what you're supposed to do. We talked about this yesterday."

"We did not talk about it yesterday!" Calm, measured George vanished in an instant. He jumped up and began to pace around. "You brought it up as I was going out the door to a meeting," he said. "I didn't get to talk about it at all!"

"You said you married me because of Ari." She wished he'd sit back down again. He made her already small room seem even smaller.

"Yes," he said tightly. "I did."

She nodded, justified. "I knew it."

"Partly," he added firmly.

She frowned. "What do you mean, partly?"

"I mean, you don't know everything." He hesitated, rolled his shoulders as if they were stiffening. His gaze flickered away, but then he brought it back to meet hers. "I married you because Ari left you…."

"Yes."

"But mostly I married you because I wanted to. I wanted you." He paused, looked straight at her unblinkingly. "I loved you."

Sophy simply stared at him.

She wondered briefly if her stiff neck had affected her hearing. If it had brought on the sudden wobbliness of her knees. She reached out and grasped the back of the chair she was closest to. It was barely enough to keep her upright. She shook her head, ran her tongue over her lips.

"No," she said. "I don't—" she began and trailed off, afraid.

"Believe it?" George finished for her bitterly. "No, I suppose you don't. I couldn't tell you then."

"When?" she said stupidly.

"When we got married. You still loved Ari and—"

"I did not!"

Now it was his turn to stare. "You loved Ari," he insisted. "You had his child. My child," he corrected firmly.

"Your child," she agreed with that much of what he said. "Ari's genes. That's all. But I didn't love him. Not when I married you!"

"But—" George said a single word of protest, then stopped.

"I did think I loved him in the beginning," she admitted. "He was a charmer."

"He was that," George agreed grimly. "No bigger one on earth."

"And no less dependable man on earth, either," Sophy said. She sighed. "I began to figure it out when he kept running off all the time. He was fun to be with when he was with me. But he never stayed. How could I love a man who didn't care about me or our child?"

George just shook his head, dazed.

"I almost didn't even go to his funeral," Sophy confided. "But then I thought I should go—for Lily. She might want to know about it when she got older." Sophy spread her hands. "I didn't love Ari," she said earnestly. "Truly. I might have thought I did once—but not later. And definitely not when we got married."

George shook his head, still coming to terms. "But you cried."

Sophy frowned. "Cried? About Ari?"

"I thought so. That first night…when we…made love."

Oh, God. Yes, she remembered those tears. "I wasn't crying for Ari. I wasn't even thinking about Ari—except maybe briefly when I thought how unlike making love with Ari was. Making love with you was…beautiful." Just like the last time they'd made love—at Tallie and Elias's. She hesitated, and then thought she had nothing left to lose and gave him the words she had been afraid to say at the time. "And I loved you."

George didn't speak. His Adam's apple moved convulsively in his throat. His fingers flexed, made fists, then opened again. He took a breath and let it out. "Then why were you so angry the next day? Why did you tell me to go?"

"I didn't believe you loved me. I thought I was a duty—one of Ari's messes you always had to clean up."

George grimaced and said a rude word. "No! I never—"

"I heard you say so, George. You told your father you'd always cleaned up Ari's messes and you were sick of doing it and that whatever it was he wanted you to do was the last one. I heard you, George, with my own ears."

"When?"

"At the christening. Upstairs. You and your father were arguing. About a woman. One of Ari's women." She forced herself to be frank. "You said you wouldn't clean up any more of his messes. And that at least he—your father—couldn't expect you to marry this one!"

"Because I was married to you!"

"Because I was one of Ari's messes!"

"No! You got it all wrong. I didn't mean you—for God's sake, how could you think it?"

"What else was I to think?"

"Not you! Not ever you! There was other stuff. Lots of other stuff. Most of my life I was cleaning up after Ari. He got in a car accident in college. His fault. He didn't have insurance. His dad had died the year before. We paid the bills, compensation, that stuff. I took care of it. My father was busy. Theo was gone. And—" he shrugged "—so I did it. Ari was the closest to me in age. We grew up together. People sometimes thought we were the ones who were brothers because we looked the most alike. There were other things, too."

"This woman?"

He shook his head. "She was claiming Ari owed her money. No, but before…there were other things…"

He was silent for so long that Sophy wondered if he would continue, but finally he did.

"He borrowed money from me when I was in grad school. He had a project that he was working on, he said. I believed him. I lent him the money. He was a smart guy, no reason why it couldn't have been a good thing…"

"It wasn't?" Sophy guessed.

George shook his head. "He'd got some girl pregnant." His voice was low, hard to hear. He swallowed. "Paid for her to have an abortion." He looked at her, his expression grim, his gaze grim. "When I found out you were pregnant, I was glad he was dead."

Sophy hugged her arms across her body. "I would never—"

"I know. I knew then. But I didn't want you to have the baby alone. I wanted to be there. Hell, from the first time I met you, I felt a connection, but how could I act on it? You were…his!"

Sophy came then and stood in front of him, looked up at him and met his gaze, stopped being afraid, stopped running. "I wasn't ever his the way I'm yours."

For a moment they just stared into each other's eyes. Then hers brimmed with tears and spilled over as he wrapped his arms around her and buried his face in her hair. She felt a tremor run through him, knew her own body trembled. Held him tight. Felt his arms crush her.

"I love you," she whispered. "I've loved you since the beginning. Our beginning. I didn't say yes so you'd take care of me. I said it because I wanted you, thought I could build a life with you, a good one, with you and me and Lily. And when I thought that family duty was the only reason you were doing it, I knew I had to let you go so you could live the life you wanted."

He drew her down onto the sofa with him and wrapped his arms around her again, kissed her cheek, shook his head. "Family duty has nothing to do with us. Never did. The life I wanted—the life I still want—is with you. Understand?"

But Sophy needed all the loose ends tied up. "What about… Uppsala? You didn't even mention it."

He shook his head. "Top secret multigovernment project. Once we got married there was no way I was going to do that. I told you that last week."

"You didn't tell me what it was," she protested.

He grinned. "Because if I did I'd have to kill you."

She grinned, too, but then her grin faded. "Are you still…?"

"No. Everything I'm doing now would bore the socks off you. But it's what I want to do—if you'll come home with me." Deep green eyes bored into hers. "Will you?"

For just a moment Sophy paused to savor the moment, to breathe in the calm and the peace and the love she'd never hoped to win. It was hers. It always had been. She regretted for an instant the time they had lost, but then thought about all the time they had left that they might never have got if these past three weeks hadn't happened.

Today was the first day of the rest of her life—and it was looking better and better.

She smiled and framed his face in her hands. "I will. Oh, George, yes, please. I will!"

They were kissing when the door opened and small footsteps came padding down the hall. "Daddy!" Lily's joy echoed around the room.

She flung herself on them and they gathered her in.

And then George pulled back. "Hang on," he said and got to his feet. Lily clung to him as he started for the door. "No," he told her. "You wait here. I'll be right back."

Lily looked disgruntled, but reluctantly went back to Sophy and crawled into her arms. Her eyes were bloodshot, too, from all of last night's crying. But her smile was real and brilliant. "I knew Daddy would come," she said.

"You're a smart girl," Sophy told her. "You believed."

Lily nodded. "You gotta."

Then the door opened again and a large exuberant black dog bounded in and leapt onto the couch with them.

"Gunnar!" Lily shrieked and threw her arms around him.

"You brought Gunnar?" Sophy stared at George, amazed. "On the plane?"

"He's part of the family," George said simply. Then he grinned and picked Lily up to find room on the sofa for all of them. "And I figured if you wouldn't listen to me, Lily and Gunnar together couldn't help but convince you." He threaded his fingers in her damp, tousled hair, making her aware of what a wreck she must look.

She said so.

George shook his head. "You are beautiful—inside and out. And I am the luckiest man in the world."

Sophy's tears spilled again. "And I am the luckiest woman."

"We are the luckiest family," Lily said. "Aren't we, Gunnar?"

Gunnar made his agreement noise and bumped Lily with his nose. She wrapped her arms around him and giggled. "Gunnar's a good brother," she said. "But I wouldn't mind one like Digger. Could I please have a brother like Digger?" she asked her parents.

Sophy looked at George. George looked at Sophy. They put their arms around each other—and around Lily and Gunnar.

Then George kissed his wife and said, "You know, Lil, that's a really good idea." He smiled into Sophy's eyes. "I think your mother and I will see what we can do about that."

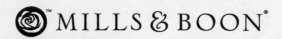

OCTOBER 2010 HARDBACK TITLES

ROMANCE

The Reluctant Surrender	Penny Jordan
Shameful Secret, Shotgun Wedding	Sharon Kendrick
The Virgin's Choice	Jennie Lucas
Scandal: Unclaimed Love-Child	Melanie Milburne
Powerful Greek, Housekeeper Wife	Robyn Donald
Hired by Her Husband	Anne McAllister
Snowbound Seduction	Helen Brooks
A Mistake, A Prince and A Pregnancy	Maisey Yates
Champagne with a Celebrity	Kate Hardy
When He was Bad...	Anne Oliver
Accidentally Pregnant!	Rebecca Winters
Star-Crossed Sweethearts	Jackie Braun
A Miracle for His Secret Son	Barbara Hannay
Proud Rancher, Precious Bundle	Donna Alward
Cowgirl Makes Three	Myrna Mackenzie
Secret Prince, Instant Daddy!	Raye Morgan
Officer, Surgeon...Gentleman!	Janice Lynn
Midwife in the Family Way	Fiona McArthur

HISTORICAL

Innocent Courtesan to Adventurer's Bride	Louise Allen
Disgrace and Desire	Sarah Mallory
The Viking's Captive Princess	Michelle Styles

MEDICAL™

Bachelor of the Baby Ward	Meredith Webber
Fairytale on the Children's Ward	Meredith Webber
Playboy Under the Mistletoe	Joanna Neil
Their Marriage Miracle	Sue MacKay

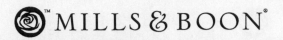

MILLS & BOON

OCTOBER 2010 LARGE PRINT TITLES

ROMANCE

Marriage: To Claim His Twins	Penny Jordan
The Royal Baby Revelation	Sharon Kendrick
Under the Spaniard's Lock and Key	Kim Lawrence
Sweet Surrender with the Millionaire	Helen Brooks
Miracle for the Girl Next Door	Rebecca Winters
Mother of the Bride	Caroline Anderson
What's A Housekeeper To Do?	Jennie Adams
Tipping the Waitress with Diamonds	Nina Harrington

HISTORICAL

Practical Widow to Passionate Mistress	Louise Allen
Major Westhaven's Unwilling Ward	Emily Bascom
Her Banished Lord	Carol Townend

MEDICAL™

The Nurse's Brooding Boss	Laura Iding
Emergency Doctor and Cinderella	Melanie Milburne
City Surgeon, Small Town Miracle	Marion Lennox
Bachelor Dad, Girl Next Door	Sharon Archer
A Baby for the Flying Doctor	Lucy Clark
Nurse, Nanny...Bride!	Alison Roberts

ROMANCE

The Dutiful Wife	Penny Jordan
His Christmas Virgin	Carole Mortimer
Public Marriage, Private Secrets	Helen Bianchin
Forbidden or For Bedding?	Julia James
The Twelve Nights of Christmas	Sarah Morgan
In Christofides' Keeping	Abby Green
The Italian's Blushing Gardener	Christina Hollis
The Socialite and the Cattle King	Lindsay Armstrong
Tabloid Affair, Secretly Pregnant!	Mira Lyn Kelly
Maharaja's Mistress	Susan Stephens
Christmas with her Boss	Marion Lennox
Firefighter's Doorstep Baby	Barbara McMahon
Daddy by Christmas	Patricia Thayer
Christmas Magic on the Mountain	Melissa McClone
A FAIRYTALE CHRISTMAS	Susan Meier & Barbara Wallace
The Soldier's Untamed Heart	Nikki Logan
Dr Zinetti's Snowkissed Bride	Sarah Morgan
The Christmas Baby Bump	Lynne Marshall

HISTORICAL

Courting Miss Vallois	Gail Whitiker
Reprobate Lord, Runaway Lady	Isabelle Goddard
The Bride Wore Scandal	Helen Dickson

MEDICAL™

Christmas in Bluebell Cove	Abigail Gordon
The Village Nurse's Happy-Ever-After	Abigail Gordon
The Most Magical Gift of All	Fiona Lowe
Christmas Miracle: A Family	Dianne Drake

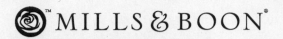

NOVEMBER 2010 LARGE PRINT TITLES

ROMANCE

A Night, A Secret...A Child	Miranda Lee
His Untamed Innocent	Sara Craven
The Greek's Pregnant Lover	Lucy Monroe
The Mélendez Forgotten Marriage	Melanie Milburne
Australia's Most Eligible Bachelor	Margaret Way
The Bridesmaid's Secret	Fiona Harper
Cinderella: Hired by the Prince	Marion Lennox
The Sheikh's Destiny	Melissa James

HISTORICAL

The Earl's Runaway Bride	Sarah Mallory
The Wayward Debutante	Sarah Elliott
The Laird's Captive Wife	Joanna Fulford

MEDICAL™

The Surgeon's Miracle	Caroline Anderson
Dr Di Angelo's Baby Bombshell	Janice Lynn
Newborn Needs a Dad	Dianne Drake
His Motherless Little Twins	Dianne Drake
Wedding Bells for the Village Nurse	Abigail Gordon
Her Long-Lost Husband	Josie Metcalfe